LOCAL HERO

Paramedic Laura Robertson has decided it's time to make a new start. She's going to move far away from her small town and leave past hurts behind. Just as she's made her decision, though, fate has one last laugh in store and brings ex-husband Fraser McCloud back into her life ... A firefighter accustomed to being the one coming to the rescue, Fraser dislikes being vulnerable. Between an injured ankle and emergency childcare duties, however, he's forced to accept help. So Laura steps in to assist ...

SUZANNE ROSS JONES

LOCAL HERO

Complete and Unabridged

LINFORD
ROMANCE

LINFORD
Leicester

First published in Great Britain in 2020

First Linford Edition
published 2021

A catalogue record for this book is available
from the British Library.

ISBN 978–1–4448–4768–0

Published by
Ulverscroft Limited
Anstey, Leicestershire

Printed and bound in Great Britain by
TJ Books Ltd., Padstow, Cornwall

This book is printed on acid-free paper

Emergency

Sometimes, Laura Robertson reflected, you could accidentally tell another person way too much when you were sitting in a parked ambulance in the dark, waiting for the next emergency. And she instantly regretted it.

'I can't believe you're leaving.' Her colleague, emergency care assistant Glenn McMillan, reacted to her shock statement. 'You've lived here all your life.'

'All the more reason to make a break for it.' She gave an awkward little laugh. 'Just keep it under your hat for the time being. I haven't even been offered any interviews yet. And I haven't told my family.' That wasn't a task she was looking forward to.

'You'll get another job no bother,' he assured her. 'They're crying out for paramedics in London. There are always adverts for vacancies. Telling your family, though,' he shook his head, 'now that's not a task I envy.'

Her smile was tense. She knew Glenn was teasing, but there was some truth to his words. There was no doubt her mother would not be impressed.

As for her sister, Flora — well, she would be excited Laura was setting out on a new adventure once she got used to the news, but would likely point out that the family would prefer her to stay.

She sighed.

She wished she'd reached this decision two years ago. If she had, she might well be living her new life by now instead of still pining over what might have been. And, by now, her family would have grown accustomed to her living away.

Not that she intended to worry about any of that tonight while she was at work. Waiting for the next call was always a tense time and she needed to keep her wits focused so she was ready to drive off at a moment's notice. There was no knowing when that call might arrive or who the next patient might be.

She peered out through the windscreen and into the dark night. Tighnamor was a quiet town by any definition. Tucked away in the north of Scotland, with a population of 50,000, there were occasions when they could sit quietly between restocking and cleaning the ambulance and the next emergency.

She knew from her limited research into the jobs market that in London it would be a different matter.

Laura squinted as something caught her eye. Something on the horizon.

She wasn't sure at first if she was imagining things. Was that an unusual amber glow in the distance? Or was it a combination of street lighting and an overactive imagination?

'What's that, Glenn?'

'What's what?'

She pointed towards the strange phenomenon.

'Over there.'

Glenn leaned forward in his seat.

'Aurora borealis?'

She'd only ever seen the northern lights in shades of green and yellow before, though she knew the aurora could present itself in a variety of colours. There was something about this, however, that worried her. The glowing seemed to be fixed over the industrial part of town and it seemed to be getting brighter.

'I think it's a fire.'

Laura pulled on her seatbelt and prepared to drive across town, just as Glenn took the call.

'We're on our way,' he told the operator as Laura steered the ambulance on to the road.

Any emergency always got adrenalin rushing though her veins — it was a crucial reaction in a race to save a life, which any of their journeys might be.

There was an added dimension to her reaction this time, though; she'd never stop feeling that cold sense of dread over her skin, or the sickness in the pit of her stomach when she was on the way to a fire.

Even though it was two years since she'd had any right to a personal interest in the safety of any of the firefighters.

'He might not even be there tonight,'

4

Glenn said quietly as they sped through the empty night-time street.

'Who might not be there?' She feigned nonchalance, but she knew she was probably fooling nobody. Least of all herself. Her hands were nearly numb with the force of her grip on the steering wheel.

'You know who.'

She resisted the urge to reply and kept driving.

'He might be your ex,' Glenn said, 'but you're still allowed to care about him.'

That was one of the major things she disliked about her hometown — the way everyone was in your business and thought they knew best.

'I care about everyone. It's my job.'

Glenn's gentle sigh signalled the end of that particular conversation and she concentrated on getting the ambulance to the site of the fire as quickly and safely as possible.

It didn't take them long, but when they arrived there were already two fire engines on the scene, along with sundry police vehicles. The siren sounds in the air warned other emergency vehicles weren't far behind.

'Looks like they're preparing for the worst.'

Glenn's words were needless. She'd already worked that out for herself. She stopped the ambulance at what she deemed to be a safe distance from the flaming warehouse, and she and Glenn both got out to see if they could help.

'What happened?' Laura asked a passing fireman.

'Not sure yet,' he called over his shoulder. 'Someone phoned it in but didn't give any details. It was already in a bad way by the time we got here.'

Laura and Glenn stood poised and ready to spring into action if they were needed.

It didn't take long for news of a casualty to filter through. A firefighter had been hurt.

Laura took a deep breath. She could feel the heat of the flames from here and the acrid smell of smoke assaulted her nostrils, but she had a job to do. So, much as every instinct warned her to run in the opposite direction, she was compelled forward by the force of her need to help.

She ran towards a small crowd of firefighters and police officers — it seemed the casualty was at the centre of the fuss.

'We carried him over — away from the fire,' Angus, a firefighter she recognised, told her. She tried to keep calm, but Angus being here meant there was a very good chance she knew other members of the crew. And one in particular.

'Let me through, please.' There was authority in her voice that disguised the dread that filled her heart. Her instincts warned her she wasn't going to like what she was about to see — and the feeling was much more than the usual sense of foreboding she experienced at this sort of emergency.

The small crowd parted, affording her a first glimpse of the man they had recently brought out of harm's way.

'Fraser,' the ex-wife in her whispered as she saw the man at the centre of the commotion. He was lying on the ground, almost unrecognisable under his protective uniform. Only she would have known him anywhere, of course. His eyes were closed and what she could see of his face was deathly pale.

Time stood still. She couldn't move or breathe. Seeing Fraser like this was her nightmare come true. He must be alive. He had to be. He was strong and fit and she refused to even think about the alternative.

Yet here he was, lying on the cold ground, not moving and surrounded by colleagues who seemed every bit as concerned as she was herself. It was almost as though she was in a parallel universe where nothing made sense.

'It's OK, Laura — it's not as bad as it looks.' Angus's tone was gentle. 'I don't think he's badly hurt. He fell off the ladder. I think he's just winded.'

Slowly that sank in. At least he wasn't suffering burns. That was something to be grateful for.

'Laura?' Glenn asked cautiously as he

stepped forward, ready to take the lead. 'Are you OK?'

The concern she heard in her colleague's voice penetrated the fear and she was galvanised into action. She'd allowed herself those moments of utter horror, but now her training took over and she became the capable professional everyone relied on.

'Is he conscious?' she asked, dropping her bag and falling to her knees beside him. His warm breath fanned her face as she leaned closer. He was breathing steadily — which was always a good sign.

As she lifted her head away from his, Fraser opened his eyes. She couldn't see the colour in this light, but she knew exactly their shade of blue. He gave his trademark grin.

Despite everything, her heart skipped a beat.

'Hello, Laura. Fancy seeing you here.' He struggled to sit up.

'Don't move until we've checked you out,' she ordered, but Fraser had never been one to take orders.

'I'm fine.'

'I think we can say he's conscious,' Glenn said unnecessarily, as he took Fraser's arm and helped him into a seated position.

Laura could happily have picked up her bag of equipment and thrown it at her ex. Or, equally, she could have hugged him. She really didn't know what to do, as annoyance that he'd frightened her so much did battle with relief that he didn't seem to be as badly injured as she'd feared.

In the end she did neither. Instead, she turned to the group that still surrounded them.

'OK, lads, Glenn and I have this.'

Everyone here knew their history and she really didn't want an audience as she assessed the injuries of the man who had once been her husband. Particularly when he was smiling at her the way he was doing now and all she really wanted to do was smile back.

The crackling of the fire raging in the background reminded her of her responsibility and she slipped effortlessly from smitten ex-wife and into her professional role.

'Where are you hurt?' she asked. 'Did you hit your head? Black out?'

She quickly ascertained that he was unlikely to be concussed, but there seemed to be a bit of a problem with his ankle.

'Can you put your weight on it?' she asked. With hers and Glenn's help, he managed to get to his feet. Or, foot, to be exact. It seemed he couldn't put any weight on his injured ankle despite his bravado. Not that he was about to admit it.

'I just need to rest it a little longer. Then I'll need to get back to the fire.'

Laura glanced around — there were at least two dozen firefighters dealing with the blaze.

'Your colleagues seem to be doing just fine without you. Besides, you'd be a hindrance rather than any help at the moment.'

'You know exactly how to make a man

11

feel special.'

She ignored the comment.

'I need to examine your ankle — there's a chance you might have broken a bone.'

'I'm wearing boots. They'll have protected my foot.'

'Boots can only do so much. Glenn, help him back on to the ground and we'll take that boot off and have a proper look.' It wasn't a good sign that the joint was severely swollen and bruised — and he winced when she applied gentle pressure to the area. 'Sore?'

He nodded.

'A bit.'

She translated that as a lot.

'Sorry, Fraser — I didn't mean to hurt you.' She closed her eyes as she realised how that might be interpreted, but he seemed to take it at face value — too wrapped up in the pain he was trying to deny.

There was nothing to indicate the bones were misaligned, so she applied a splint, ready to transport him to hospital.

'I'd like to take you to get that x-rayed,' she told him, preparing for an argument.

Fraser had never been one to show weakness or to enjoy a fuss whenever he'd been unwell. And even tonight, when there was no doubt he was in a lot of pain, he was likely to still put up a fight against accepting help. He didn't disappoint.

'I'm fine, Laura. I'll put a packet of frozen peas on it when I get home. That should sort it out.' He looked as though he meant it, too.

Glenn laughed at that and she tried not to join in — she didn't want to laugh when he'd been hurt — but she felt the corners of her mouth curve upwards at the reminder of just how stubborn he could be.

'You haven't changed.'

He gave an exaggerated frown.

'Given that you left me, I take it that's not a compliment.'

'Not even close,' she told him lightly, although she'd rather die than let him see that his comment hit home.

She didn't need a reminder of the fact she'd left him, thank you very much. It was never very far from her thoughts even after all this time — that was the reason she'd decided to leave town.

'What do you think, Glenn?' she addressed her colleague while all the while being unable to take her eyes from Fraser. 'Will we haul him on to the bus, kicking and screaming?'

Given he was six foot four, it would have been a difficult job for anyone to manhandle Fraser into the ambulance against his will, but she had to make a stand. If he went against advice now and there were bones broken, they could lead to problems for him in future.

'How did you even manage to fall off the ladder in the first place?'

'I didn't fall. I stepped off awkwardly.'

'OK — how did you manage to step off awkwardly?'

He gave an easy shrug, not at all offended by her tone.

'These things happen,' he said, his grin making her heart leap again.

She took a deep breath before trying again to persuade him to see sense.

'Fraser, it really would be sensible to get checked out.'

He gave a brief nod.

'OK, if I need to, I'll go and get an x-ray later. But at the moment you can't tie up an ambulance transporting someone with a twisted ankle. You need to stay around in case you need to deal with a real casualty.'

At that moment, there was a loud crash from the warehouse as the fire continued its trail of destruction and reminded them all of just how dangerous the situation was.

She knew he was right. Even though she was worried about him, even though she knew there would be more paramedics along at any moment, they didn't know what tonight would bring. Experience told her they might be faced with many more casualties before dawn finally broke.

'How about I ask if one of the police officers could run Fraser to A&E?' Glenn asked. 'I just overheard the DCI saying they would be sending some of them back to the station in a minute. They could drop him off at the hospital on the way.'

Yes, that might work. She looked to Fraser to see if he might bring up any new objections, but he quietly nodded.

'OK,' he said.

'All right then, Glenn. That would be a good idea. Thanks.' Laura would have preferred to take Fraser herself, but as long as he got to hospital, what did it matter how he got there? Or who drove him?

Fraser McCloud meant nothing more to her these days than any other patient.

She just had to keep telling herself that.

* * *

Fraser wasn't quite sure what had happened. A missed rung in the midst of all the heat and smoke and shouting as he'd stepped off the ladder and landed badly. The pain had seared through him instantly, making him feel dizzy. His confusion had been further compounded by his colleagues acting quickly and lifting him out of harm's way.

Though none of that had anything to do with the way his heart had leapt when he'd spotted Laura. At first, he'd thought he was dreaming — the sickening crunch and pain from his ankle as he'd landed had been pretty overwhelming and he wasn't sure if he hadn't passed out.

But when he'd realised she was real, her face had made him forget his discomfort for a moment and nothing else had mattered.

Though he was quite annoyed she'd made him come here, to A&E.

'I feel a fraud,' he told the doctor as she examined his x-ray. 'I'm wasting your time.'

'Well, you needn't and you're not. It's broken.'

Knowing he'd be in a cast and unable to work for at least six weeks made it even more annoying that Laura had been right. But then she usually was.

'We'll get an ambulance to take you home once we've sorted you out,' the doctor added.

He didn't even have the energy to fight that offer. He was exhausted. Not least because seeing Laura again had brought back memories he'd rather not dwell on. He still missed her, even two years on.

'No need to arrange an ambulance, doctor. I'll take him home.'

His head snapped round so fast he was surprised he didn't add a whiplash injury to his list of woes. Had his thoughts conjured her up again? Or had Laura, judging by her jeans and T-shirt, now off duty, really come to pick him up?

The sudden wave of light-headedness that hit him was down to the painkillers he'd been given, he was sure — rather than because of the smile that would possibly have knocked a lesser man off his good foot.

A Lift Home

'What happened at the fire after my undignified exit?'

They were waiting for painkillers to be sent up from the pharmacy and he tried to keep the tone light, though he needed to hear her answer. He was worried. There might have been causalities. It had been a nasty incident.

Her smile, unbearably sweet even after a twelve-hour shift, put his mind at rest.

'They managed to get the fire under control before I was off duty. No other casualties, but the building's beyond repair.'

Buildings were replaceable — people weren't. This scenario was the better of the two options. The enquiries and the piecing together of evidence would start as soon as possible, he knew. The best they could hope for was that it had been an accident. Though the spectre of wilful fire-raising couldn't be discounted.

He shuddered. Just the thought that

someone might have put so many lives in danger on purpose angered him.

'Cold?' Her brown eyes were wide with concern and his heart contracted.

How had he managed to let things go wrong between them? Why had he ever let her go?

'No, I'm fine.'

'These chairs will be playing havoc with your back. You've been sitting down for hours. Will I go and see what the hold-up is?' She was on her feet and looking for someone to ask before he could stop her.

It had been a long night and an even longer morning. They were both exhausted, but in all honesty, he would have happily sat here all day if it meant spending more time with her. The prospect of going back alone to his empty house was even more depressing than his broken ankle.

Laura obviously worked her charm on whoever she spoke to. Only minutes after she'd left she arrived back at his side, and his medication arrived in her wake.

'Any pins and needles, any swelling in your foot, or if it turns blue, then you need to see a doctor.' The final warning rang in Fraser's ears as he was finally allowed to leave.

Negotiating his way to the car park proved more difficult than he'd expected. Walking with a cast and on crutches always seemed so easy when he'd watched others do it. It took all his concentration, but he was still aware of Laura walking by his side, carrying the bag of painkillers the hospital had sent him home with.

'Let me get the door for you.' Laura unlocked the car, then opened the passenger door wide — taking the crutches from him as he settled himself into the seat.

He hated that he was in a position to need help, but if he was going to accept assistance from anyone he was glad it was Laura who had stepped up. Being with her seemed right and natural and he closed his eyes, for just a minute, wallowing in her nearness as she drove him home.

'Come on, sleepy head. We're here.' He heard her voice from far away. 'Fraser?'

He awoke with a start — disorientated and confused by the sound.

'I'm sorry,' he said, sitting up, the throbbing in his ankle reminding him of why he was in her car. 'I must have dropped off.'

The mid-morning sun was shining on her hair, turning it to copper. Fraser knew exactly how soft it would feel in his hands — the fresh smell of the shampoo she liked to use. He allowed himself to be dazzled by his memories for just a moment before harshly reminding himself he had no right to think about Laura's hair in any context these days.

'Understandable, given you've been working nights and it's now nearly lunchtime,' she reminded him. 'Not to mention the hours of sitting around at the hospital.'

She rushed to help him out of the car. 'I'm too heavy for you,' he said as she reached in for him. He tried to grab his crutches from where she'd rested them against the side of the car and struggle up without her help. And he failed miserably.

'Why are you so stubborn?' She shook her head. 'I'm a professional. I do this sort of thing all day, every day. Let me help you, Fraser, before you do yourself another injury.'

'I feel like such an idiot.'

She looked surprised.

'Why on earth?'

'Well, it's not even a proper injury, is it? It's just my ankle. It's all my own fault — a moment of stupidity where I rushed ...'

'So you'd prefer to have been seriously hurt?' He could see the disapproval in her eyes and recoiled from it. 'Just so you could boast about some manly accident?'

'Not exactly.' He grimaced. 'I just feel such a fraud, using up resources at the hospital. Taking your time up.'

'Don't be so daft. None of us mind

that. We just want you to get better — and to make sure you don't try to do too much and hold your recovery back.'

His embarrassment had compensations, Fraser realised, as he took one crutch from her and allowed her to put her arm around his waist to help him to the door.

Her touch reminded him of everything he'd lost — and it was oddly addictive. He couldn't have stepped away even if his ankle had allowed it.

He'd expected her to drop him off at the door and rush off back to her own place. He wasn't the only one who'd been working nights. But she surprised him by coming into the house with him.

This was the first time she'd been back here since the divorce and he wondered how she must be feeling. It must be odd for her — as it was for him. Her expression gave nothing away, though.

'Are you hungry?' she asked.

'No.' His stomach chose that moment to rumble loudly. 'Yes,' he corrected, with an embarrassed grin. It had been a long time since that hurriedly grabbed sandwich at the hospital that one of the nurses had fetched for him from the canteen.

Laura smiled.

'I'll see what I can rustle up.'

He knew he should tell her he could take care of himself. That she needed to go home and rest. But the chance of having her here even for only another few minutes was too much to resist.

She belonged here. With him. Even if fate had decided otherwise.

'You don't have much in,' she told him when she came back a short while later with two plates. 'All you had in the fridge were some eggs, so I've made Spanish omelettes with veg I found in the freezer — including that bag of peas you were going to use on your ankle.' She gave his cast a wry look and he squirmed a little.

'Sorry. I haven't been shopping yet this week.'

She frowned.

'Well, I wouldn't make any plans to go anytime soon. You heard what the doctor said about resting that ankle.' Then her expression softened. 'I need to get a few bits myself, I'll pick some stuff up for you at the same time and drop a bag off before work tonight.'

It was on the tip of his tongue to tell her not to. A broken ankle wouldn't stop him placing an order online. But his sleep-deprived cognitive skills finally sprang to alertness and he realised that if she did his shopping she would have to come back.

And much as he didn't want to put her out, his need to see her again — like this, where they were comfortable with each other — was stronger.

'That's good of you. Thanks, Laura.' He grinned as he picked up his fork and started to eat.

And it was the most delicious omelette of his life.

★   ★   ★

Being back here was surreal. She'd lived here with Fraser for the whole of their

26

married life — and she'd lived in her own place without him for two whole years.

Stepping back into this kitchen, though, for the first time since she'd moved out, brought a whole host of unwelcome memories crashing down on her. The reasons she'd left. The way things had fallen apart.

But there were some good memories, too. They had laughed a lot. And sometimes it was good to look back on that — though in the old days there had always been plenty of food in the cupboard, and they had both enjoyed cooking for each other.

He seemed impressed enough by her effort today, though, and smiled across at her as he tucked in.

'How's the ankle feeling?' Laura asked, her concern breaking into the easy silence.

'I'll live,' he assured her unnecessarily.

And she was reminded again of the fear that had gripped her before she'd discovered his injury wasn't life threatening. Pushing the recollection to one side, she made a conscious effort to divert the conversation to a safer topic.

'How will you fill your time for the next few weeks if you can't work?' She knew he still played rugby in his spare time, but that would be off the agenda for a while.

He grimaced.

'I'm going to look on the bright side. There are a couple of books I've been meaning to read for a while now. And some films I've been keen to watch.'

She smiled.

She couldn't see it, somehow. Yes, he had been known to sit still, and even occasionally pick up a book, but Fraser was a large, athletic man. He was going to go crazy cooped up in the house on his own, day in and day out.

'Maybe some of your friends will visit,' she suggested.

'Maybe,' he agreed as she took his empty plate. 'Leave the dishes on the side — washing up will give me some-thing to do when you've gone.'

When she'd gone. She tried not to

react.

She didn't want to leave him, but she'd need to be away soon — it was getting too cosy here and she could easily slip back into domesticity with Fraser. His company was too familiar, his home still too much hers.

She stacked the dishwasher despite his instructions, knowing his balance would be compromised while he got used to the cast and crutches.

He didn't need to be bending down to stack plates — he'd probably end up head first amongst the saucepans.

Really what she had wanted to suggest was that she would call by to keep him company. It would be pushy to suggest it, though.

And it would definitely not be a good idea for an ex-wife to assume such a responsibility. No matter how much she might want to. They were supposed to be moving on with their lives apart from each other. There was no way they could do that if she was hanging around his place all the time.

If nothing else, this was proving her decision to move away was the right one — for both of them.

The doorbell interrupted her walk back from the kitchen to the living-room.

'I'll get it,' she called, knowing he'd be struggling to get up.

When pressed, the doctor had admitted moderate exercise would do no harm as long as he didn't overdo it, but there would be time enough for him to do that when he'd rested and the shock of his injury had worn off.

Angus stood on the doorstep and offered an uncertain smile.

'How is the invalid?'

'Doing OK, but I know he'll be glad to see you.'

She preceded Angus into the living-room.

'You have a visitor,' she told Fraser unnecessarily as his friend walked in.

'So what's the verdict?' Angus asked as he sat down.

'It's a fuss about nothing,' Fraser insisted, downplaying the fact he'd actually broken a bone.

Laura shook her head. If she hadn't seen for herself just exactly how much pain Fraser had been last night, she might very nearly have believed this story now. As it was, she was in no mood to listen to entertain him being flippant.

He'd been very lucky last night. She knew how much worse an injury to a firefighter on duty could be. Even more, she'd spent too many years worried about what could happen to Fraser while he was on duty.

She knew humour and trivialising the situation was his typical way to deal with any sort of crisis.

She shook her head in exasperation.

He grinned.

'What?'

'I'll be off, then.'

Fraser raised an eyebrow at her clipped tone. Angus, not knowing her nearly so well, noticed nothing amiss and waved a hand in farewell.

'Goodbye, Laura,' Fraser eventually said. 'And thank you for your help.'

She nodded in acknowledgement.

'You'll excuse me if I don't see you out?' he called after her as though he couldn't help it.

Everything was a joke.

To be honest, in her line of work she and her colleagues often used humour to deflect the horrors of the situations they were sometimes called to deal with. It was just this time she was dealing with Fraser.

And even though she recognised things could have been much, much worse, for those moments when she'd first seen him lying on that cold, dark ground, time had stood still.

With a sigh, she put her car into gear and drove away.

She was tired, but too restless after everything that had happened to go straight home.

She toyed with the idea of shopping now, but as she drove past her sister's house, it was obvious Flora was home — her car was in the driveway, and windows were open to let in fresh air.

The twins would be at school at this time of day, and she knew Flora would probably be working, but on impulse, she stopped the car anyway.

Her sister worked from home, and Laura generally didn't make a habit of intruding on her time during the working day.

As a widow with young twin daughters to take care of, she knew Flora had set up her business so she could work around her girls. She couldn't afford to be distracted during the hours they were out at school.

But it had been a tough few hours, and Laura really needed her sister's sympathetic shoulder today.

'Do you have time for a quick coffee?' she asked when Flora came to the door.

At one time, Fraser would have been the one who knew Laura better than anyone else. These days, however, Flora was the one she felt comfortable turning to in a crisis.

Flora took one look at Laura's face and opened her arms to embrace a sister in a warm hug.

'That's good timing,' Flora said, seeming to know there was something the matter without even having to ask. 'I was about to take a break.'

Laura followed her sister inside, and waited until they were both settled at the kitchen table with mugs of hot coffee before she related recent events.

'I heard about that fire on the news.' Flora took a sip of her hot drink. 'They mentioned a fireman had been injured, but I had no idea it would be Fraser. Is he all right?'

Laura nodded. The professional front that had kept her together during most of last night and this morning completely deserted her, and the sting in her eyes warned that tears weren't far away.

'I'm sorry,' she said, as she began to sob.

'Oh, darling, give me that coffee and I'll put some sugar in it. It will be the shock. It does funny things to you.

'And it can't have been easy to have seen Fraser lying on the ground like that, even if you are no longer together.'

Laura didn't stop Flora from heaping generous spoonfuls of sugar to the drink and stirring.

Sweet drinks and foods were her downfall. Under normal circumstances she tried to be healthy and kept to a strict diet — but there was nothing normal about today's circumstances. And, as she sipped the sweetened drink, she did slowly start to feel more like herself.

'Sorry, Flora. I don't know what came over me there.'

Flora arched a knowing eyebrow.

'Don't you? Really?'

Laura gave a grimace.

'OK. Maybe I do know. His injury isn't serious, but I didn't know that at the time.'

Flora shook her head.

'I don't know why you two can't just work something out. You were made for each other.'

Laura kept quiet. Over the past two years, Flora had been very vocal with her opinions and attempts to discover why

Laura and Fraser had parted.

Flora was gazing expectantly at her now, probably thinking she might get answers while Laura was feeling vulnerable.

Laura was tempted to offer her planned move into the equation to throw Flora off the subject of Fraser.

However, given Flora already looked as though her head might explode with opinions which would go unheeded, she decided it was probably not a good idea. Her sister might not be able to deal with the additional whammy.

'I've said it before, and I'll say it again,' Flora added for good measure. 'You and Fraser should be trying to sort things out.'

'What I should be doing,' Laura said, forcing a bright expression, 'is leaving you in peace to get on with your work.' She got to her feet and took her mug over to the sink to wash it up.

'If I didn't have a deadline to tie up those accounts, I'd be forcing you to stay and talk it through.' She followed Laura to the door.

'I'll get Mum to look after the girls this evening, and I'll pop by yours with a bottle of wine. We can have a proper chat then.'

'Aw, that's lovely of you, but you don't need to do that. I won't be around this evening in any case. I'm on duty.'

'Well I'll forget the wine and pop by at teatime, then.' Flora wasn't giving up. 'Mum will be happy enough to feed the girls — she's always offering.'

'Really, Flora, it's fine.'

'I'll cook for you before you head off.'

There was nothing else for it. Flora wouldn't take no for an answer so Laura was going to have to fess up.

Laura took a deep breath.

'I'm going to have to go shopping before work. I told Fraser I'd pick up some groceries for him.'

'Did you?' Flora brightened up at that prospect. 'That's excellent.'

'It's just shopping.'

'Of course it is.'

'I'm just helping out a friend.' Laura's attempt to defuse any suggestion of rekindling her romance with Fraser fell flat. That much was obvious by the grin on Flora's face.

'If you say so.'

Time to go — before her sister accused her of protesting too much.

On the drive home her mind buzzed with it all — the feelings that had nearly floored her when she'd discovered Fraser had been hurt, the memories that had surfaced when she'd spent time with him in the house that had once been theirs ...

Reluctantly, in the deepest part of her mind, she finally admitted she wished she'd done more to keep the marriage together.

Checking Up on Fraser

Laura's head buzzed with wishful thinking and might-have-beens. By the time she got home she was sure she'd never manage to sleep.

Exhaustion caught up with her pretty quickly, though, and, before she could think of anything else she was jolted suddenly awake by the blasting of a car horn outside.

There was still plenty of light coming through the cracks in the curtains and she could hear the reassuring sounds of traffic coming from the main road that passed by her flat. She was still tired so it surely couldn't be time to get up yet.

On a whim she reached for her phone to check the time — to see how much longer she had to sleep before her alarm rang.

Her eyes focused on the numbers and she sat bold upright, heart beating madly against her ribcage. She'd forgotten to set her alarm before nodding off. It was nearly five p.m. She knew a few moments of utter panic. She had so much to do before her shift started.

Then she realised her own shopping could wait until tomorrow. All she needed to do was have a quick shower, and she would still have time to dash to the supermarket to pick up some things for Fraser.

She knew he'd understand if she phoned and explained that she couldn't pop by this evening, he could even do an online order, but he'd had so little in the cupboard when she'd made their omelettes earlier, she hated to think he might go hungry.

Three quarters of an hour later she was on his doorstep with a couple of shopping bags, but he wasn't answering the bell.

Trying the handle, she discovered the door was unlocked, so she stepped inside — and nearly collided with him in the hallway.

'Steady,' she warned as he wobbled precariously.

For a moment their eyes met, and her heart skipped a beat.

The old magic was still there.

She coughed in an attempt to dispel the sudden awkwardness.

'What kept you?' she joked, trying to keep things as normal as possible.

He gave a mock frown, obviously quite happy to play along.

'Give a man with crutches a chance.'

'You shouldn't have left the door unlocked,' she told him as he struggled to turn his large frame around in the limited space of the hallway. He was way too close. 'I could have been anyone.'

He glanced over his shoulder, made eye contact, and grinned.

'Worried about me, Laura?'

Of course she was worried about him. Tighnamor was fairly safe as towns went, but the thought that he was lying injured, his reactions dulled by painkillers, and someone might wander in while he was unable to defend himself scared her witless.

'I would be concerned about anyone

in your position.'

But, specifically, she was worried about him.

'And there was me thinking I was special.'

She bit her tongue. Flippancy seemed to come so easily to him. Had he really moved on as completely as he appeared to have, or was this a front to hide the fact that the past still hurt?

She followed him through to the kitchen, where she held out the bags of shopping. He glanced pointedly at the crutches.

She didn't budge.

'You have to learn to adapt and work with the injury,' she told him, 'and do things for yourself. Lean one of the crutches against the worktop, and then you'll be able to put the shopping away.'

'You're too cruel.'

'Cruel to be kind.'

It was hard to watch him struggle. But necessary. She knew that she would be doing him no favours in the long run if she mollycoddled him. No matter how much she might want to.

Tough love was difficult to dish out, though.

* * *

'How is he?' Glenn asked when she arrived for shift that night.

She didn't pretend she didn't know who he was talking about this time. There was no point when most of their friends and neighbours would soon know she'd spent most of her waking day taking care of him.

'Getting used to moving around on crutches.' She smiled.

'Was it broken?'

She nodded.

Glenn shook his head.

'I don't envy him. He'll be off work a while. And he won't be able to play rugby, or go walking, or climbing.'

Glenn wasn't telling her anything she hadn't already worked out for herself, but hearing it from her colleague reiterated the negative effects the injury would have on Fraser's life. If only in the short term.

'He's clung on to the doctor's lower estimate and hopes to be fine in six weeks or so.'

'Hopefully he will be. He's healthy and if there are no complications, maybe he'll be lucky. He'll need plenty of visitors to keep him from getting bored, though. Is anyone staying with him? His sister?'

No-one had been there when Laura had popped by earlier, but maybe he had made plans.

'I don't think his sister will be staying — not at the moment. She's got the baby,' Laura reminded him. 'And I think she's on her own just now. The last I heard her husband was working away.'

No, Kim definitely had enough on her plate without taking on care of her brother.

'Besides,' she said, 'he'll be fine once he's used to getting around.'

And she truly believed that. He'd always been the more organised one in their relationship. Laura was sure he wouldn't have changed in that respect.

'Did you tell him you're moving away?'

She sighed.

'I did not. I'm not telling anyone else at the moment — I told you that yesterday.'

It wasn't often she felt irritated with Glenn. He was an easy man to get along with, but right now she cursed that easy manner that had coaxed that particular piece of news from her.

'And don't you go spreading it around before I get a chance to tell people myself.'

'OK, OK. I'm sorry.' He held his hands up in mock surrender as they walked to the ambulance. 'I was only asking.'

She hadn't meant to snap at Glenn, but he had brought up a thought that hadn't occurred to her before.

Maybe she would have got away with it if their paths hadn't crossed again, but now she would have to tell Fraser she was leaving. It was only right. But the prospect of doing so filled her with even more dread than even the thought of telling her family.

She had time, though. She'd only just made the decision and she didn't even have another job lined up yet.

'Enough chatter.' She smiled to soften the blow of her sharp words. 'Time we hit the road.'

It seemed to be one thing after another on the shift that night. An elderly lady with asthma was quickly followed by a toddler with an elevated temperature and a rash, and then a middle-aged man with a suspected heart attack. All were dropped, in their turn, to be checked out at the hospital.

Then there was a call from a worried passer-by to check on a young man who had collapsed on the street in the town centre. This part of town had been pedestrianised.

Laura hated driving down there, particularly at this time when some of the locals would have been in the pubs for hours and would have spilled outside to mill around.

Keeping her wits about her, she slowed

to a crawl, but kept the lights flashing. The crowds parted before her, but she didn't increase the speed. You never knew with people — especially when someone had taken a drink.

'There he is,' Glenn called as Laura navigated the ambulance down the cobbled high street. There was a small cluster of people to the left of them, all visible on this dark night thanks to the street lighting.

'He's fine,' his very merry friend assured them. 'He's just been celebrating. Needs to sleep it off, that's all. He was promoted at work today.'

Laura quickly checked pulse and breathing. All seemed good. She hoped for the young man's sake that his boss never saw him in this state. It was obvious from the smell of his breath that his particular brand of celebration had involved large quantities of alcohol.

'What's his name?'

'Ian,' the friend replied. 'Ian Smith.'

'Ian,' Laura called. 'Can you hear me?' There was no response. The boy was out cold.

'There's a nasty gash on his head,' she said. 'Did he hit his head when he fell?'

'No. Yes. Maybe.' The boy shrugged. 'I don't know.'

They obviously weren't going to get much sense from his friend, so she and Glenn loaded Ian Smith into the ambulance to be checked out at the hospital.

'Is there a full moon behind those clouds?' Glenn joked after they had safely dropped the young man at the hospital.

Laura smiled. It was a well-known phenomenon in emergency circles that shifts were much busier when the moon was full. She completely blamed that on better visibility and more people out and about causing trouble rather than on any supernatural lunar properties.

The rest of the night carried on in the same way — and she was grateful for that. It meant that she had no time to think about a certain ex-husband. Or to tell Glenn more than she intended to about her plans — as she had the night before.

She and Glenn were exhausted by the end of the shift.

'It will be ten times busier in London,' he warned her as they took the ambulance back to the station.

'Good,' she said. 'That's exactly what I need.'

She needed to be so busy that she didn't have time to think about the life she would have left in Tighnamor. Or the man she would have also left behind.

'Want to go and get some breakfast?' Glenn nodded towards the café that was across the way from the station.

'Not today.' She wanted to go and see how the invalid was. Even though it was early and he might still be asleep — and even though she knew realistically he had to be OK. He was a grown man and it was only his ankle, for goodness' sake.

She just needed to see him — and any excuse would do.

She'd bought fresh pain au chocolat — his favourite breakfast, or at least it had been when they'd been married — and cups of freshly brewed coffee from the baker's across the road from the station.

Once Laura got to his house she sat in the car for a while, looking up at the home where she'd once been so happy. They'd moved in here as newly-weds. They'd had so many dreams for their shared future.

She couldn't quite believe it had all fallen apart.

Leaving without checking on him would be the sensible thing to do. It wasn't as though he didn't have other people who cared.

There was Angus, for a start. The fact he had been around yesterday to check up on Fraser proved he was someone to rely on. Then there was Kim — the woman who had been Laura's friend when they'd been sisters-in-law.

She didn't see much of Kim these days. Maybe an occasional glimpse in the street as each pretended they hadn't seen the other as they went about their business.

That was only natural in the circumstances. Lines had been drawn. Sides had been chosen. And, even though neither she nor Fraser had technically done anything wrong, it had become awkward for their friends and family.

But Kim would be there for Fraser if he needed her, Laura knew.

She sighed.

Fraser didn't need her. His life now was none of her business. He was better off without her. And letting him become a part of her life again would be dangerous for both of them.

And yet, although she knew she could drive away, she found herself getting out of the car.

Fraser drew her towards him by some intangible force. He always had.

She tucked the bag with their breakfast under one arm, then balanced the cup holder in the same hand, and managed to press the doorbell. It took him a while to open the door.

He smiled when he saw her and her heart knew at once that she'd done the right thing — even if her head had been screaming no.

He looked dishevelled, his blond hair in need of a comb. But he was dressed so had obviously been up and she was glad she hadn't woken him.

'I brought breakfast.' She held up her early morning purchases like a champion displaying a medal.

'Well, I wasn't expecting this.' Fraser had balanced both crutches under one arm so he could open the door and he used his free hand to push it closed again, before he struggled to readjust the crutches and followed her through to the kitchen.

'I couldn't let you starve.' She put the pain au chocolat on to plates, and took the coffee cups out of the holder.

'That was hardly going to happen. You brought me a ton of shopping just last night.'

Laura smiled. She'd been rumbled. Fussing over him wasn't something an ex-wife should be doing.

'Ah, yes, but I didn't bring you any pain au chocolat. Or fresh coffee.'

'I'll get fat if you keep feeding me up like this.'

'You might.' She smiled at the thought. Fraser had never had to worry about his weight and she knew, once he was back on his feet, he'd work off any extra pounds this enforced rest might introduce. His sports and his hiking had always kept him fit and active.

At one time Laura had gone with him when he'd hiked in the hills around Tighnamor. She closed her mind to the memory of happier times.

'It's just one breakfast,' she added for good measure.

Their eyes met for just a second, before he grinned back and her heart fluttered.

He was an action hero. He raced into fires, he rescued people from blazing buildings, he had even been known to rescue the odd kitten from various plights. The law of averages meant that it had only been a matter of time before something happened — he was high risk.

And who could stop themselves from falling for a man like him? Not her, that was for sure. But Laura still knew she'd done the right thing leaving him. They hadn't been good for each other.

'You're too good to me.' He bit into the pain au chocolat.

She winced — it was almost as though he'd read her mind.

'Yes,' she agreed. 'Yes, I am.' Though what else was she supposed to do?

What she wanted to do was to gather him in her arms, to keep him safe, and to make the pain in his ankle go away.

The reality was, she was no longer entitled to do the first, and the second and third things had always been beyond her capabilities.

She had to keep reminding herself of that.

'How are things with Kim?' she asked. She still cared about her ex-sister-in-law — even if their friendship had been sacrificed at the altar of the divorce court.

He nodded.

'She's good. You heard she and Matthew had a baby?'

'Yes, I saw the announcement in the

local paper.' She took a sip of her coffee. 'A little girl, wasn't it?'

'That's right. They called her Grace.' Fraser's eyes lit up as he spoke of his niece. 'She's amazing. Just a bundle of cuteness.'

Laura had seen Kim in town, pushing a pram, a few months ago, but hadn't managed to get close enough for a peek at the baby.

'Has Kim heard about your accident?'

He nodded.

'She came over yesterday.'

Laura nodded, her mouth too full of the delicious melt-in-the mouth pain au chocolat to reply.

'Matthew's away, and she suggested I could go and stay with her and Grace,' he said, between bites.

'Why didn't you?' Was it rotten of her to be glad he hadn't gone? Probably. But she wouldn't be able to go and visit him if he was staying at Kim's.

'You're as bad as she is.' He laughed. 'It's just my ankle. Once I get into the habit of using these,' he leaned across from his chair and tapped his crutches, 'I'll be fine. Besides, she said she was going to pop by again this morning.'

He seemed bemused by the fuss, but he would need help, Laura knew that. He wouldn't be able to drive, for one thing.

And, as Glenn had helpfully pointed out, he needed company. She knew he'd go mad if he was cooped up on his own in the house until the cast came off. But she wasn't about to argue with him about it. She'd leave that to his sister.

'Where's Matthew these days?' Laura asked about Kim's husband. 'Is he still working abroad?'

Fraser nodded as he leaned to take her now empty plate and stack it with his own on the table.

'Bolivia. Something to do with a silver mine.'

As a geological engineer, Matthew travelled the world lending his expertise wherever it was needed. Kim had travelled and worked with him before she'd had the baby. But, of course, Laura had lost track of the couple's whereabouts when she'd stopped being a member of their family.

'And Kim's managing without him?'

'Like a trouper.'

Laura knew she should leave. They'd finished their breakfast now. She really had no excuse to linger. She got to her feet.

'Thanks for breakfast.' His smile was as it had always been. All crinkly eyes and sunshine.

And, just as she always had, she smiled back.

★ ★ ★

'Laura was there?' Kim's eyes were wide as glanced up from feeding mush to baby Grace. 'Why didn't you tell me this yesterday?'

'She was the first paramedic on the scene.'

He knew instantly that he shouldn't have told his sister that his ex-wife had effectively picked him up off the ground. The instinct that had made him keep the fact quiet yesterday had been right. She would read far too much into it. She was already reading too much into it. He could see that in her expression.

But she would find out eventually, no doubt. And she would read a good deal more into the situation if she discovered he'd kept that very important fact from her.

'How is she?'

'Fine.' Understatement of the century. She was a whole range of adjectives that all amounted to a lot more than fine.

'And she took you to hospital?'

He shook his head.

'I hitched a lift in a passing police car.'

Kim looked appalled.

'She would have taken me,' Fraser rushed to explain, 'but I couldn't allow an ambulance and experienced crew to be diverted from a serious fire just for an ankle injury.'

She nodded.

'Laura came to the hospital after her shift, though, and drove me home,' he added.

Kim's lips settled into a tight line.

'You should have phoned me. I would have collected you.'

'I know you would, but it was very early and you have Grace.'

'Babies are portable, you know. And she has a car seat.'

'If I'd been stuck I would have phoned you, but it was fine.' She didn't need to know he would have phoned for a taxi rather than put her out.

Kim didn't seem convinced.

'How did you feel, seeing her again?' She wiped the baby's mouth with her bib as she waited for Fraser to reply.

'Strange. Almost as though the past two years hadn't happened.'

'Well, they did,' Kim snapped as she whipped the bib away. 'She hurt you really badly when she left you. Don't forget that.'

He wasn't likely to. He carried the ache of missing her around with him every waking moment.

'She was hurt, too.'

'That wasn't your fault.'

'It wasn't hers, either.'

'Maybe.' Kim sighed loudly as she got to her feet. 'You need to let Laura go and move on with your life. Make sure you don't let yourself go down that road again.'

'I won't,' Fraser assured his sister. Though it wouldn't be out of choice. Laura wasn't coming home, he knew that in his saner moments. But, whenever she'd fussed over him over the past few days, he couldn't help imagining a different future. One where he wooed her back. And one where they were happy and grew old together.

He knew it wasn't going to happen, but he was allowed to dream. Wasn't he?

News From Bolivia

Fraser thought over Kim's words after she and Grace had left. He knew his sister was right. There had been a lot of arguments towards the end of his marriage. And even more unhappiness after it was all over.

Letting go was another matter, though. Deep in his heart, he knew he hadn't done enough to stop Laura from leaving. And, if he was ever lucky enough to be given another chance, he'd do things differently and somehow convince her to stay.

The morning stretched out ahead of him after his sister had gone, but despite that in the end it passed in a blur.

For a man who wasn't able to get around much, he was kept busy. Word had spread about his accident and, between phone calls and impromptu visits, he didn't have much chance to be bored or lonely.

Though the one visitor he really wanted

to see stayed firmly away — which he really shouldn't complain about. She'd already been to visit once today — and after a busy night at work, too.

When he'd opened his eyes after he'd hurt his ankle at the fire and had seen her staring down at him, her face pale and her dark eyes wide, he'd thought the pain had knocked him out and he was dreaming. But it had all been too real and he had felt foolish that such a silly accident had made him weak and vulnerable.

Not that Laura had worried about that — she'd been more concerned with providing medical treatment, than she had about the fact her ex-husband had made a fool of himself.

She'd been efficient and professional, and he'd never been prouder of her — despite the fact he had no right to that emotion.

A sudden knock at the door startled him.

More visitors.

'It's not locked,' he shouted, knowing

he should make the effort to move, but not quite able to bring himself to.

Oddly, after hoping she'd turn up all day, he hadn't really been expecting her to. When she appeared at the living-room door, it was a surprise.

'Hello.' He smiled and his breath caught when she smiled back.

She stepped further into the room and sat in the chair closest to his.

'You look completely fed up.'

He had been. But not so much now that she was here.

'I'm fine,' he said.

'Have you been out today?'

He shook his head.

'That's what I thought. Grab whatever you need, and I'll take you for a run in the car.'

His first thought was one of pure joy. Not necessarily at the prospect of getting out of the house — though that was very tempting — but at the thought of spending time with her.

Even if they hadn't been able to live together, she'd always been his favourite person. The divorce and time apart didn't seem to have changed that.

'Do you have time? Don't you need to get ready for work?'

Laura shook her head.

'I'm not on duty tonight.'

The prospect of an evening with his ex-wife made his heart leap.

'Let's go,' he said, needing no coaxing now to struggle to his feet. Despite his eagerness to get out, his movement through to the hall was laborious and he was grateful for her help with his jacket.

He was pleased, though, that he managed to get into her car with minimal help this time. After the fuss last time, at least he managed to regain some dignity.

'You're already getting more mobile,' she commented in response.

'I could hardly have got any worse,' he pointed out with a grin.

'You could have fallen flat on your face,' she suggested. Her tone was light, but then she shuddered. 'I shouldn't even joke about that.'

Fraser sat back and it wasn't long

before she drove on to the road that would take them both out of town.

'Where are we going?' Why hadn't he thought to ask that before? He had put himself in her hands with blinding trust.

She glanced across at him.

'Dancing.' Her expression was deadpan, but there was a hint of mischief in her eyes.

He laughed. Dancing was what he hated most in the world, mainly because he had no sense of rhythm, but he still could think of nothing nicer than taking her in his arms, holding her close, smelling the scent of her shampoo as they moved around some hypothetical dance floor to some imaginary love song … ankle injury or no ankle injury.

He was almost disappointed as she turned the car down the narrow lane that headed out towards the loch. Almost.

Once Laura had parked the car in the tiny car park, she rushed around to his side of the vehicle and opened the door for him, holding his crutches ready as he struggled to get out.

65

It was good to be out in the open air again. Surreal. But good. Being cooped up indoors even for just one day didn't suit him.

Fraser breathed in the fresh air as he followed Laura down to the water's edge and they settled on a bench there.

She was so close he could have easily reached out and taken her hand. He thought she might let him, too — she seemed to have softened towards him since the accident.

The itching brought him sharply to the present and he waved an arm to try to disband the swarm of insects who were intent on turning him into their supper.

'Midgies getting to you, McCloud?' Despite his efforts to play it cool, she'd obviously noticed his discomfort.

Fraser slapped his hand against his face to dislodge the midge that seemed to be feeding there.

'Nothing I can't handle.'

'I can take you home if it's too much for you, tough guy?'

He was tempted. Despite his initial

gratitude to be out and about, home sounded very appealing. But then if he asked her to take him home, she'd drop him at the house and be on her way. He was sure of it.

'It's starting to get dark in any case,' Laura added.

There was no doubt the sun was setting rapidly, but he still wanted to linger a little longer.

'No, you're all right. We can stay and enjoy the view just a bit longer.' He'd prefer to be eaten alive by midges, if it meant he would be able to spend a few more minutes with Laura.

Reluctantly, she settled back down beside him on the wooden bench, and stared out towards the water.

'Maybe we could do this again some-time? Once my ankle's healed.'

The words were spoken quietly, but she couldn't miss the hint of hope. Hope that deep in her heart she wanted to encourage, but that couldn't allow to flourish.

'Fraser ...' She let out a sigh. 'I think

you should know that I'm planning to move away from Tighnamor.'

The words hung in the still night air. Immediately she wished she hadn't blurted the news out like this. But she'd had to say something. He was bound to find out eventually, and it wasn't fair for him to hear it from a third party.

And it definitely wasn't fair for her to allow him to hope a reconciliation might be possible.

'Where are you going?' His voice was hoarse, the tenderness of only a few minutes ago replaced by a tone of disbelief.

'London.'

'Seriously?'

She nodded.

'You'll hate it.'

'Perhaps.' She knew she would — if only because he wasn't there. But moving away was to be her version of ripping off a sticking plaster. For past hurts to heal she had to suffer a little immediate pain.

'When are you going?'

'As soon as I find a job.'

He seemed to relax then.

'So it's not definite?'

'It's definite. I've made up my mind.'

Spending this time with him was reminding her of the good times they'd shared. But there had been bad times, too. That was why she had left. If she was to have any hope of starting over, it was more important now than ever that she get away. If she allowed herself to fall for him again, she might never get over him a second time.

'Don't go,' he said.

Laura gave in to the urge that had nudged at her since they'd sat down and she covered his hand with her own. It felt good and she couldn't believe that something so natural could be a mistake. Fraser didn't pull his hand away.

'I have to.' It was obvious to her now that he hadn't moved on, either. She had to sever ties, to make a new life, for his sake — and that was a much more powerful motivator than doing it for her own sanity. They hadn't been good for each other.

'It's the right thing to do.'

Fraser said nothing. But he turned his hand over beneath hers, and his fingers curled tightly around hers. Almost as though he thought that by holding her hand tightly, he might be able to keep her from going.

Laura wished more than anything that things were different and that they had been able to live happily together and that she hadn't made up her mind to leave.

* * *

Fraser sat up half the night, wondering what he could have said to persuade Laura to stay in Tighnamor. What he could say the next time he saw her that might persuade her.

He even rehearsed a few arguments in his head. Her work, her family, they were all important to her.

Over and over the words went through his mind as he waited the next day for her to arrive. She hadn't promised she'd pop in, but it seemed he was taking it for granted that she would.

The hours ticked by, and when there was no sign of her he knew he'd completely ruined whatever slight chance there might have been of persuading her to give their relationship another chance.

The day took for ever to drag by. News of his accident was old hat now and the flurry of visitors that had beaten a path to the door yesterday were now satisfied he was OK.

No doubt Kim would pop in at some point, and possibly Angus would visit, too, but people were busy with work and their own families.

Fraser wondered if he should phone Laura. He needed to apologise for speaking out of turn last night.

He knew her shift pattern meant she would have a few days off. But he kept putting the call off, knowing it was wrong to deny that he still wanted her to stay in Tighnamor — even if he had no right to stand in the way of her dreams.

His ankle began to throb merrily,

warning him it was time for a painkiller.

He'd struggled into the kitchen and was holding a glass under the running tap when he heard the front door being opened. Hope fluttered to life in his chest, only to be dashed when his sister walked in, baby Grace in her arms.

The baby gurgled when she saw him.

'Hello.' He smiled, happy to see them, despite the fact he'd hoped Laura had come back, and the baby smiled back, all gums and sunshine. A stark contrast to the worried frown on Kim's face. 'Are you all right?'

She didn't speak, but sank down into a chair at the kitchen table, her face paler than he'd ever seen it.

'Kim, what's the matter?' Getting worried now, he hopped over and pulled out a chair and sat beside her. 'What's happened?'

'It's Matthew,' she whispered. 'The mine collapsed. He was on site at the time.'

His intake of breath was sharp, even to his own ears.

'Is he OK?'

She shook her head.

'They don't know. They haven't been able to make contact with anyone inside the mine yet.'

This didn't sound good. Matthew's work could be dangerous, that was understood. But to hear he'd been involved in an accident like this had caught Fraser unawares and it was obvious his sister was in shock.

'I have to go to him.' Kim hugged her baby tightly and kissed the top of Grace's head.

'You're going to Bolivia?' Matthew had left his wife and daughter behind in the Scottish Highlands as the mine was remote and no place for a young family. The thought that Kim would take Grace out there at this time when the situation had the added complication of missing — possibly injured or worse — personnel was worrying.

She looked at him.

'What else can I do?'

'Stay here and wait for news.' It seemed

perfectly reasonable to him. She had the baby to think of. There was no way she could easily take Grace all that way, particularly with the knowledge Matthew had already deemed the environment unsuitable.

'I can't just sit here and do nothing.'

'So you're going to go over there and do nothing?'

She shrugged.

'At least I'll be there when …' She took a deep breath. 'When he's rescued.'

Fraser said nothing. He hoped the outcome would be positive, but there was no denying it might be bad news. And how would Kim cope then, with a small baby, miles from home, and with nobody to support her?

It seemed her mind was made up, though. If it wasn't for his ankle, he'd insist on going with her, but with his mobility issues he'd only add to her problems.

'I have to go,' she said desperately, he suspected, more to convince herself than him.

He could talk her out of it, but he knew that if he did, he'd have to live with the consequences. And if the worst happened she'd never forgive him for interfering. However much of a mistake he thought it might be, he had to support her decision to go.

'At least leave Grace,' he suggested. 'Travelling all that way with a small baby isn't going to be ideal, and the mine is remote, you'll be miles from anywhere — shops, medical help if Grace was ill — it wouldn't be safe for a baby.'

Kim was thinking over his words, he could see from the frown on her face.

Eventually, she shook her head.

'I can't. Matthew will want to see her when he's pulled out.'

'You don't know what conditions you'll have to stay in.'

'We'll manage somehow.' And then the clue she was seriously considering his suggestion: 'Besides, who would I leave her with?'

'Me.' He could see the incredulity in her eyes and he knew at once what she must be thinking. 'It's just my ankle. I can feed a baby and change nappies no bother.'

'Are you sure you'd manage?'

He smiled reassuringly.

'Are you seriously asking me that? I'm an emergency worker. I put out fires and rescue kittens. Taking care of one tiny human being for a few days isn't going to tax me too much.'

'What if it's more than a few days?' She bit her lip.

As a professional firefighter, he wasn't in the business of offering false hope to anyone. However, as a brother, it was a different matter.

'There's a good chance they'll have dug him out before you even land.'

She gave a brief nod.

'Go and fetch Grace's things,' he urged. 'And I'll go online and book your flight.'

A Practical Arrangement

Grace was a joy and a delight, but Fraser had seriously underestimated the amount of work required to successfully look after a small human being. Kim had barely left in a taxi to the airport, and he was already slowly drowning under all the paraphernalia she'd insisted the baby needed. Not to mention the constant treadmill of jobs that seemed to be on a repetitive loop.

One gummy smile from his niece, though, and his mood was instantly restored. And looking after the baby made him forget, for a while, that he wasn't able to work, or go hiking, or play rugby. In short, she was a full-time job in a floral romper.

He glanced at the clock.

'It's only been an hour since Mummy left to catch her plane,' he told Grace in mild surprise.

The baby gurgled happily, not at all concerned that the laws of time and physics seemed to have slowed beyond all recognition.

Then she promptly brought her lunch up so Fraser had to rush, as far as he was capable, to fetch one of the many bags Kim had brought, so he could change her into fresh clothes.

When the doorbell rang he was glad of something so normal.

'It's open,' he called, none too loudly so he didn't frighten the baby.

It seemed he hadn't frightened whoever was on his doorstep, either, because a few moment later, the bell went again.

'It's open,' he called again, louder this time. Grace screwed up her face and began to bawl.

He didn't know if his visitor had heard or not and he didn't much care. The baby was distressed beyond anything in Fraser's limited babysitting experience, and he jiggled her up and down, trying to soothe her distress.

'Well, I wasn't expecting to see a scene of such domesticity.'

He turned and grinned at Angus, glad

to see another adult, even if the baby in his lap was still screaming.

'I seem to have frightened her.'

'Not surprised, with your face.' Angus picked up a rattle that Kim had left and began to shake it, to try to distract Grace.

It worked surprisingly quickly. The baby reached out and took the toy, her recent fright at Fraser's raised tone in answer to the ringing of the doorbell seemingly consigned to the past.

'I didn't know you had a way with babies,' Fraser told his friend.

'Me, neither.' He looked a bit alarmed, maybe worried word would get out and his hard-man act would be rumbled.

Or maybe he was worried Fraser might ask for help with babysitting.

'Take it that's your sister's baby?'

Fraser nodded.

'This is Grace. Kim had to go away, so I said I'd mind her. It's not like I've anything else to do for the next few weeks.' He quickly brought Angus up to speed with recent events.

'But you have a broken ankle.'

He shrugged.

'What was I supposed to do? I couldn't let Kim down.'

Angus grimaced supportively.

'I'll go and put the kettle on, will I?'

'That would be great.'

'How long's Kim away for?' Angus asked as he put a mug of strong tea down within reach of Fraser — but far enough away so that there wouldn't be any accidents with hot liquid near the baby.

He gave Angus the edited highlights of his brother-in-law's plight.

'There are a dozen men trapped underground. They've yet to establish contact.'

Angus shook his head, obviously considering what he'd been told with the mind of a professional emergency worker.

'That doesn't sound good. Was it wise for her to go out there on her own? I mean, what if it's not good news?'

'I know. That's worried me, too. But she wouldn't be told — she was desperate to go, even though there was nobody to go with her. And she's a grown woman, so I couldn't insist she wait here for news, even if I am her brother.'

'She was always a bossy one,' Angus said, smiling fondly, no doubt remembering the time Kim had shouted at both of them for walking into her kitchen with muddy boots.

'Older sister's prerogative. And at least she left Grace with me. The mine's in a very remote location and Matthew had told her conditions weren't brilliant. It would have been asking for trouble taking a baby.'

'Well I hope it turns out well for Matthew.'

'Me, too, Angus.' Hope was all they had now. 'Me, too.'

* * *

'Auntie Laura, can we have some chocolate, please?'

Laura looked down into two pairs of pleading brown eyes and wondered why she thought it would be a good idea to

81

bring two six-year-olds to the super-market.

She should have waited until Flora came home from her exercise class. She could have easily popped in on her way home with much less fuss than she was currently experiencing.

'Girls, you know your mother wouldn't like it.'

Their faces fell and Laura felt dreadful. She hated denying her nieces anything, but she really couldn't go against Flora's wishes.

'Mum likes chocolate, too,' Amelia's small voice offered hopefully.

With a sigh, Laura ignored the giant bar the girls had been eyeing up and came up with a compromise.

'OK, why don't you choose some nice chocolate and we'll buy it for her as a present. She might let you both have a piece after you've eaten your tea.'

The girls cheered, and Laura smiled, all the while hoping her sister wouldn't be too cross. She loved this time with her nieces every week while Flora went to the sports centre, but they were already running rings around her. She suspected she was too soft with them. But then, wasn't that a favourite aunt's job?

'They sound happy,' a masculine voice sounded behind her.

She turned warily. She didn't recognise him at first, which was odd as she'd known him for years, both as Fraser's friend and as his colleague. It was because she was seeing him out of context, she supposed.

'Hello, Angus.' She smiled at her ex-husband's friend.

It was funny, she'd managed to keep away from Fraser and his circle for a good deal of the past two years, but since his accident, she seemed to be destined to keep bumping into them.

And the questions burning on her tongue, conjured up at the very sight of his friend, were about Fraser. Had Angus seen him today? How was he doing? Was Kim looking after him?

Laura stopped herself before the words could be formed, but this was yet another reason it was a good idea to move away.

She'd been living in this half-world too long. A new start with new people would maybe mean she'd be able to put her past behind her without thinking — hoping — she might bump into Fraser. Or any of Fraser's friends so she could pounce on any relevant snippet of information from them.

'You seem to have your hands full.' He nodded towards the girls, who were now eyeing up extremely large boxes of very expensive chocolates.

'My nieces,' she explained.

He gave a short nod.

'Seems to be mind-a-niece day in Tighnamor today.'

What was he talking about? Something of her confusion must have shown on her face, because he rushed to explain:

'Fraser,' he said. 'He's taking care of Grace.'

Laura felt her eyes narrow.

'What do you mean?'

'Kim's had to go away, so Fraser

stepped in to help.'

Laura nodded. That sounded like the sort of thing Fraser would do.

'Where's Kim gone?'

'She's on her way to Bolivia.'

She felt the shock right down to her toes.

'Bolivia? So Fraser will have Grace for longer than just this evening?' She knew he was capable and dependable, but she knew enough to realise babies were hard work — and he wasn't used to taking sole care of a small human being.

And then there was the problem of his injured ankle …

'She'll be staying with Fraser until Kim gets back.' Angus spelled out the situation, which was just as well because Laura was having difficulty believing it.

'Bolivia?' she said again. Something from a world news report she'd listened to earlier jolted in the back of her mind. 'A mine collapsed there today. Don't tell me Matthew's involved.'

'He's missing,' Angus told her, his expression grave. 'We're hoping for the best. Though I don't understand what Kim thinks she can do by going all the way over there.'

Laura's heart went out to Kim. She could understand why Kim had gone. It would be for the same reason she herself kept going back and see how Fraser was doing.

Only Kim had been forced to leave her baby behind, and Kim's marriage was still intact. So really it wasn't the same thing at all.

It was much worse.

★ ★ ★

Fraser was looking particularly fetching in the varying degrees of white that flecked his fair hair and most of his clothes when Laura walked in. He was sitting at the table with the baby in his lap and a tiny yoghurt container discarded in front of them.

Had one pot of yoghurt really gone that far? Or had he opened a second?

'You are aware that you're supposed

to feed that stuff to the baby, not bathe in it?' She hoped her flippant tone would divert his attention away from the fact that walking in here and seeing him with a baby had nearly floored her. Particularly as Grace looked so very like her uncle, with startlingly blue eyes and fair hair.

Fraser gave a start and turned. He smiled when he saw her.

'I didn't hear you come in.'

'Sorry, I should have knocked.'

He smiled.

'You never need to knock at my door,' he told her.

Laura watched as he used Grace's bib to gently wipe around the baby's mouth.

She still didn't quite know what to say. The family resemblance was astounding. And, before she could stop herself, she found herself wondering if their baby, if they'd stayed married long enough to have one, would have looked like this one.

Her sharp intake of breath had him looking up.

'Are you OK?'

She nodded, her eyes still on the baby.

'She looks like you.'

'Not surprising. We're related.'

Laura pulled out a chair and sat down.

'How are you managing?'

His smile was wry.

'Given that it's only been a few hours, surprisingly badly. I thought it would be easy. Grace isn't even walking yet, but there's an awful lot of fetching and carrying to do for someone so small and I'm still finding it a bit awkward getting around.'

Laura reached out gently touched Grace's chubby little hand. The baby's fingers curled instantly around hers and her heart lurched. Despite everything, she found herself smiling at the child, the gesture widening as Grace responded and smiled back.

'You're just the most gorgeous thing ever,' she told the baby, who chatted back in the most charming gibberish.

'Can you keep an eye on her while I fetch a cloth?'

Before waiting for an answer, he handed the child over. And Grace felt right in her arms.

Laura was aware of a huge fuss as Fraser struggled to his feet and grappled with his crutches. She should offer to fetch the cloth herself — but he needed to learn how to move, she reasoned. Her motive for staying seated, though, had nothing to do with Fraser's best interest this time, and everything to do with the way she couldn't tear herself away from the baby.

But if she kept telling herself it was for Fraser's own good, she might begin to believe it . . .

Fraser knew he should fetch himself a clean top while he was up off his chair, but his clothes were upstairs, and it seemed like more trouble than it was worth for the moment. Instead, he grabbed a handful of sheets of kitchen paper and dabbed furiously at the yoghurt Grace had managed to knock off the spoon and on to his person.

Then he prepared the baby's milk —

exactly as Kim had shown him before her hurried departure — and checked it wasn't too hot or too cold.

'Do you want to give her this?' he asked Laura tentatively, holding out the baby's feeding bottle.

Instantly she froze, her expression unreadable. He wondered if he'd said the wrong thing. Maybe the gesture hadn't been appreciated.

Then she reached out, her fingers grazing his as she took the bottle.

Grace snuggled in her arms and Fraser made himself and Laura a cup of tea before sitting back down beside her and Grace. By which time, the baby had finished drinking her milk.

The two were the picture of contentment, a soft smile playing on Laura's lips as she gazed at the baby in her arms, Grace's eyes heavy as she nestled close against Laura.

'I should go,' she said. But she didn't move and Fraser guessed she wanted to leave as much as he wanted her to go. Which was not at all.

'Stay and have your dinner with me.'

She looked up, the expression in her dark eyes made his breath catch. Then she nodded.

He wished it had always been that easy to persuade her to stay.

Laura sat cuddling the baby while he made dinner. There wasn't much movement needed between fridge, cooker, and sink. And it was only boiling up some fresh pasta and adding a pre-prepared sauce.

He would have liked to have made her a better dinner — something special — but it was probably best not to push it until he was surer on his one good foot. Besides, he was getting around much better now. In the house, at least.

His niece was fast asleep in his ex-wife's arms by the time the meal was ready. Fraser took a moment to absorb the scene — torturing himself with thoughts of what might have been. But then she looked up, maybe she'd sensed his eyes on her, and he quickly recovered.

'Do you want to put Grace in her

travel cot while you eat your meal? Kim set it up in the living-room.'

It was pretty obvious that was the last things she wanted to do, but she reluctantly got to her feet — careful not to disturb the sleeping baby in her arms — and went through to the living-room.

'I've only just thought … How are you going to manage with the baby and the stairs? You can't possibly carry her up and down — not with your cast and crutches.

'And you can't leave her to sleep down here alone. What if she cried in the night? It would take you too long to reach her.'

Those same thoughts had occurred to him already — and he had it covered.

'I'm going to sleep on the sofa.'

She glanced at him, no doubt confirming his six foot four frame in her mind. Then she shook her head.

'You can't sleep on the sofa.'

'Why not?'

'Just look at you. You'd never fit on it. You'd end up with all sorts of aches and pains. And your ankle wouldn't be properly supported.'

That was true. His ankle ached enough as it was in the morning — he imagined the pain would be worse if it had to dangle off the end of the sofa overnight.

He shrugged.

'I'll make up a bed on the floor, then.'

Laura looked appalled.

'You can't sleep on the floor.'

'Why not?'

'Well, you just can't.' She frowned.

'We're agreed I can't sleep upstairs, not with Grace down here. And it wouldn't be an option to keep carrying her up and down the stairs when, to be honest, I'm still struggling to get myself up and down them. So sleeping on the floor is the best option.'

'It would be cold.' She shuddered. 'And uncomfortable.'

'I've no choice. Unless you have any other ideas.'

'Maybe I do.' She hesitated, seemingly torn about sharing this bright idea of hers.

Fraser raised an eyebrow, hoping to

coax her revelation along.

'I have a spare bedroom,' she revealed, 'with a comfortable bed. Why don't you and Grace come and stay with me until Kim gets home?'

For a moment he was speechless. That was the last thing he'd expected.

He didn't like to accept help, he didn't like being vulnerable. And he'd been telling the truth when he'd said he was happy to bed down on the floor. But the next best thing to having his wife here at home with him was for him to go and stay with her.

Laura knew it was the kind thing to do, to offer to help him under the current circumstances. There was a selfish element to her offer, though, that made her ashamed of herself.

The thought of Fraser staying in her home appealed more than it should have done. Despite the fact their marriage was long since over and bringing him in under her care would be taking a step back for both of them.

But as she looked at his face to try

to gauge his reaction, and his slow grin made her heart skip a beat, Laura knew she'd have made the same offer a million times over.

'OK,' he agreed easily.

Laura lived in a flat on the third floor. But there was a lift. And, once inside, everything would be on one level. Much easier for him to negotiate than the current upstairs downstairs arrangement he had to deal with.

And, when she wasn't working, she would be on hand to help.

'When can we move in?'

Fraser's words brought home the enormity of her offer.

What had she done?

She knew a moment of panic as she realised the implications. There would be another break up. When Kim came home and claimed her baby, Fraser would have no reason to stay.

But she had made the offer now.

'No time like the present.' She sealed her fate with a decisive tone that masked the hesitation in her head — even if her heart rejoiced. 'My next shift's not until next week, so I'll be around to help you settle in and make sure you have everything you need.'

Fraser reached for his phone.

'I'll see if Angus is around to help us fetch and carry. I'm not going to be much use in that department, and while I can travel light, we'll need to bring the baby's stuff.'

Laura looked around at the bags and equipment Kim had brought to her brother's house, then she smiled.

'Yes,' she agreed. 'I can see Grace is high maintenance.'

Babies always were. She had once considered hiring a truck to transport all the paraphernalia Flora had needed on a day out for the girls.

'But when you're as cute as Grace,' she added with a smile, 'you get away with anything.'

Moving In

Fraser collapsed on to the sofa as soon as they got to Laura's place. She glanced across. His face was pale, and there were lines of tension on his handsome face.

'When did you last take one of your painkillers?' She suspected, in all the excitement, he must have forgotten.

'I'm trying to wean myself off them,' he replied.

She wasn't convinced.

'If you're in pain, you need to take something. The doctor didn't prescribe them for fun. Where are they?'

She was aware of Angus's surprised look. Maybe it wasn't seemly for an ex-wife to be nagging her ex-husband about his medication, but she was a professional. She didn't like to see anyone in pain.

And, if she was a little fussier about Fraser taking his medication than she have might have been about a random patient, then that was nobody's business but her own.

'In here.' He wearily patted his jacket pocket.

'Good. Look after Grace for a minute and I'll fetch you some water.'

It was a measure of how much she wanted Fraser to take his tablets, to make sure his pain eased that she handed the baby over to him so easily. Without Grace her arms felt empty and cold.

'I'll leave these here,' Angus said, putting down the cot and the bag he carried as she headed for the kitchen. Laura cast him a grateful look. They might have managed without him, but the move would have been more difficult and taken a lot longer.

'Thanks, Angus,' she called over her shoulder. He'd disappeared by the time she came back with a glass of water — no doubt fetching the next load from his car.

Laura took Grace back from her uncle, so he could take his painkillers. The baby gurgled approvingly at this new pair of arms offering cuddles and

Laura laughed as chubby little hands reached out to pull at strands of hair that had escaped her ponytail.

'Look who I found downstairs,' Angus called from the open doorway where he stood with another armful of stuff from his car.

Laura turned her head and was shocked to see Flora standing there, the girls on either side of her. The look on her sister's face betrayed a similar emotion as she took in the scene in Laura's flat.

Then Amelia and Jessica ran over to make a fuss of Grace, both reaching out and giggling as she held on to their outstretched hands. Flora, though, stood rooted to the spot, her mouth agape.

'They're only staying for a few days,' Laura felt compelled to say. 'Just until Kim gets back. Fraser was going to find it difficult to manage the stairs at his place, what with his ankle and Grace.'

She was babbling. And Laura could see from Flora's expression that her sister was bursting with curiosity. She braced herself for an interrogation.

'I wonder if you could do me a favour?' Flora said instead, the strain of reining in her need to know showing in her tense little smile.

Laura heaved a sigh of relief. She knew the questions would come, but was grateful Flora had decided that this was not the time or the place. Not now, with Fraser within earshot.

That was one thing Laura hadn't counted on in her hasty invitation to Fraser — having to explain to her family that he really was just a friend and that there was absolutely no chance of a reconciliation.

'Of course. What do you need?'

'Someone to watch the girls for an hour.' She looked around at Fraser, Grace, then at the bags that littered the floor. 'Though it looks like you've got your hands full. I can take them to Mum's.'

'Aw,' came a dual chorus of complaint. 'We want to stay with Auntie Laura and the baby,' Amelia added, just in case the message hadn't been received.

'It's not a problem,' Laura insisted.

'I need to drop some files off with a client and I'd prefer not to take the children.'

'It's fine,' she said again, conscious of the baby yawning sleepily in her arms. 'Just pick the girls up whenever you're ready. We'll get on fine, won't we?' She grinned encouragingly at her nieces, who obliged by cheering.

Flora gave one last look at Grace, made an obvious show of holding her tongue. Then she nodded.

'Thanks. You're a lifesaver.' She came over and kissed both her girls. 'Be good for Auntie Laura.'

'We will,' they chorused.

Flora grinned at Grace, then smiled warily at Fraser.

'I hope they won't disturb you too much.'

'Not at all,' Fraser replied easily.

'I'll walk you to your car,' Angus offered, having offloaded another assortment of bags. 'I've got another load to collect. One more trip should do it.'

Laura knew she should put the now-sleeping Grace down so she could go and help. But he seemed to have it all in hand. Besides, with the baby so comfortable, she was reluctant ever to let her go.

'I'll set the cot up,' Fraser said.

And once it was done, she had no excuse. Her arms felt immediately empty. She wanted to pick the baby up again. But she couldn't disturb her.

By then, Angus was back with the last of bags.

'Cup of tea?' she asked, reckoning that was the least she could offer.

'Great. Thanks.'

She made tea for the adults and juice for Amelia and Jessica. Soon they were all sitting around in her sitting-room.

'Whose baby is Grace?' Amelia asked.

'Is she yours?' Jessica chimed in.

'Don't be silly,' Amelia told her sister. 'It takes ages to have a baby.'

'Grace is my sister's baby,' Fraser told them gently. 'Auntie Laura is helping me look after her while her mum and dad are away.'

The girls seemed satisfied with that and turned their attention to drinking their juice.

'It was good to see Flora.' Angus took a gulp of his tea. Laura winced. It must still have been boiling hot. 'I haven't seen her for a couple of years.'

That was around the same time Laura and Fraser had parted.

'How is she doing?'

The question was casual, but Laura hadn't missed the spark of interest in his eyes as he'd glanced at Flora earlier. Her sister hadn't been out with anyone since she'd been widowed — which was understandable when she'd been so busy looking after her twin daughters and trying to run a business.

But it had been a while now. Perhaps it was time she dated. Even if nothing came from it, Angus was a good guy and it would be good for her sister to do something fun for once.

She smiled, wondering how she could go about playing matchmaker.

'She's fine. She went thought a bit of a rough time of it, but she's building a new life for herself and the girls.'

Would it be overkill to add how the family hoped she'd meet someone, she wondered? Probably. This needed delicate handling.

'Is she seeing anyone?' Angus negated the wondering — again with that casual tone. But Laura was sure there was more to it. And when she glanced across at Fraser, she could see his eyebrows disappearing into his hairline.

'Not at the moment.' That, she decided, was far more encouraging than telling Angus the truth — that Flora hadn't looked at a man in two years. That would only frighten him off. 'Not at the moment' gave the impression her sister was open to the thought of meeting someone.

* * *

'What was all that about?' Fraser asked as he hobbled back into the living-room after seeing Angus to the door. The girls had gone through to watch a film on the TV in Laura's bedroom, Grace was fast asleep in her travel cot. They were effectively alone now.

Laura couldn't help smiling.

'It seems there might be romance in the air.'

'Really? Is Flora interested in him?'

Laura shrugged.

'She doesn't seem to be interested in anyone. But Angus seems interested in her and she could do worse.' She was thoughtful for a minute.

'Do you think we should play Cupid and help things along?'

The idea wasn't one she relished. She didn't like to meddle in other people's lives. But she wanted her sister to be happy. And, while she knew Flora was coping just fine on her own, there was more to life than just coping and managing.

It was years since her sister had had

someone to spoil her and cherish her and make a fuss of her. Every woman deserved that once in a while.

The thought occurred that the same thing could apply to her, but she quickly told the voice to be quiet. She really was fine on her own.

Fraser shook his head.

'Angus is a big boy. If he wants to ask Flora out he'll do it without any help from us.'

She mentally crossed her fingers that he would. And that Flora would say yes.

* * *

Kim phoned while Laura was in the kitchen, tidying up after Angus had left. She didn't mean to eavesdrop, but it was impossible not to hear — sound travelled in this place.

'Grace is in good hands.' The words were spoken with firm authority and hopefully they would have reassured Kim.

From the tone, Laura suspected Fraser's sister was none too happy.

It must be horrible for her. So awful to have had to leave Grace. Additional worry being mixed into the pot was in nobody's best interest.

She said so when she went back to join Fraser in the living-room.

'She's not worried about Grace,' he admitted. 'It's me she's concerned for.'

'Because of your ankle?'

'You'd think, wouldn't you? But no. She thinks you're going to break my heart again.'

The words were so softly spoken that she might well have imagined the 'again'. But she knew she hadn't. She had broken his heart — and her own — and that was something she would have to live with.

'You can tell her from me that I promise to leave you alone.' She tried to keep the tone light-hearted, but the joke fell flat.

Fraser didn't even make a pretence of laughing.

Fraser had known as soon as he'd stepped over the threshold of Laura's flat that this was a mistake. This place was unmistakeably hers — her things all around, her perfume in the air.

Making a clumsy attempt now to change the subject, he recognised one of the figurines on the mantelpiece and hopped over to pick it up.

'I won this for you,' he said. He remembered that day so well. It was only a chalk figure, but she'd taken a fancy to it and he'd thrown hoops at a stall when the funfair had visited town.

'I know. I was there.' She smiled at the memory and he wanted to gather her in his arms and hold her close.

The buzzing of the entry phone stopped his thoughts from wandering into dangerous territory. He was almost glad when Flora walked in shortly after. This was too confusing.

He'd jumped at the chance to stay with Laura, but maybe he should have been more cautious. Maybe Kim had been right. Maybe he was risking his heart again. But maybe she was worth it.

'How was your client?' Laura asked her sister.

Flora grimaced and perched on the sofa next to her sister.

'In a panic about his tax. His own fault — he's so disorganised.'

'Does he have anything to worry about?' Fraser asked, fascinated by this insight into a small business. He was glad he was salaried, his tax deducted at source, and he didn't have to worry about such things.

'No, of course not. I wouldn't work for anyone who was dodgy.' She seemed affronted and he wondered if he should apologise. But then she smiled.

'But he's getting a tax inspection tomorrow and it's always disconcerting when someone goes through your finances. How have the girls been?' she asked, looking around. 'And where are they?'

'They've been angels, as always,' Laura

declared and smiled as Flora rolled her eyes in mock disbelief. 'They're watching a film. I'll go and tell them you're here.' She got up and soon Fraser was on his own with her sister.

'What's really going on here?' Flora asked as soon as Laura was out of earshot.

'Laura's helping me out. It was her idea.'

'Do you think it's a good one?' She didn't look cross or unkind, but a worried frown creased her brow.

'I hope so. I don't think I would have managed without her.'

Flora nodded, but didn't look convinced. Before she could say anything else, the girls rushed in and piled on to her lap and the three all dissolved into fits of giggles.

He'd forgotten that about Laura's family — how they liked to laugh. At one time he'd been included in that laughter. Not any longer though. As Laura joined in, he was reminded again that he was an outsider in her life now.

'OK, girls.' Flora struggled through the tangle of limbs. 'Time we left. It's getting late. She smiled at Laura and then at Fraser. 'Thank you so much for minding them.'

'No problem,' Laura said, cuddling the nearest twin and kissing her head. 'You know it's always lovely to see them. Even if they are monsters.'

The girls made a feeble attempt at complaining about the label foisted upon them by their aunt, but it wasn't long until they were laughing all over again.

★ ★ ★

It was a conversation that was bound to happen from the moment Flora walked in and found the scene of domestic bliss. Laura wasn't at all surprised when her mobile buzzed shortly after she'd gone to bed and the display revealed it was her sister calling.

'You weren't asleep, were you?'

'No, I was reading. I always find it difficult to adjust after being on nights.'

'So Fraser and Grace are staying with you now?' Flora wasted no time in getting to the point.

'They are.'

'How long for?'

'Just until Kim comes back. You heard about Matthew?'

'I think everyone in Tighnamor has heard. But I still can't believe you think it's a good idea for Fraser to stay in your home. With his baby niece. Not if you're as adamant as you told me about not getting back together with him. Don't you remember how upset you were when you broke up?'

Laura sighed into the phone.

'I couldn't just leave him to struggle on his own.'

'But there must have been someone else who could have stepped up to help.'

'Who? You know there's only the two of them, that's why Kim had to leave Grace with him in the first place. If there had been someone else, don't you think she would have asked them? She knew Fraser would have trouble getting around with his ankle.'

'And there's no chance of the two of you getting back together?'

'None.' Laura had made up her mind. Two years ago they had wanted different things from their marriage, and there was no evidence to suggest Fraser had changed his mind.

'Then you're playing a dangerous game.'

'I know.' There was no denying it.

'You know nobody would be more delighted than me if you and Fraser got back together.' She carried on as though Laura hadn't spoken.

'But if you're sure that's not what you want then you're asking for trouble. And what happens when he and Grace leave?'

She knew Flora wasn't trying to hurt her, but she might as well have punched her.

'I can handle it. I won't get too close. I know what I'm doing.' But the thought of them leaving made her heart lurch.

But she and Fraser hadn't been able to live together before, and there was no reason to believe that had changed.

Just as well she had made plans to move away.

She was yet to hear anything from the flurry of applications she'd sent away, but surely it was only a matter of time before she was invited for interview.

And, once that happened, she'd make sure they would find it hard to turn her down.

Her escape route was already plotted.

This time when she and Fraser parted, she would be fine.

Interview

Almost as though Laura had willed it through her need for an escape plan, an e-mail arrived the very next morning — inviting her to attend an interview for a job in London. She considered telling Fraser over lunch, but she remembered how he'd reacted the last time she'd talked about moving away and she didn't want to ruin the perfectly lovely meal he'd prepared.

Instead, she hugged the secret to herself and eventually confided in Glenn, as they sat in the ambulance on their next shift a few days later.

He let out a long sigh.

'I didn't think you were really serious about going.'

Laura shrugged.

'Seems I was. Though it's only an interview — I haven't been offered another job yet.'

'Of course they'll make you an offer. It's a foregone conclusion, someone with

115

your skills and experience.'

'I hope you're right.'

'I'm going to miss you,' Glenn told her, in rare serious mode.

She smiled.

'I'll miss you, too. But you'll find someone else to work with.'

As would she. But it wouldn't be the same. She and Glenn were good friends and she would have to be very lucky indeed to find another work partner who was as compatible.

A call to a road traffic accident took Laura's mind off her own problems. The public reacted to the lights and the siren and the traffic before them magically parted to let them through.

Luckily, it was a minor incident. Everyone insisted they were fine and, after quickly checking them over, Laura and Glenn had to agree.

'Wish all our calls were that easy to deal with.'

Laura nodded. Some of their calls were challenging to say the least.

'Do they have any idea what caused

the fire up at the warehouse?' Glenn asked, and she was glad that he changed the subject.

'There was apparently another fire in the same area last night,' she said. 'Angus phoned Fraser this morning to let him know. It's starting to look like it might be deliberate, but investigations are still ongoing.'

She and Glenn hadn't been on duty, but it seemed another firefighter had been hurt. This time the injuries sustained, while not life-threatening, were more serious than Fraser's. She was going to be in hospital for a while.

* * *

Fraser's motives for agreeing to move in with Laura might have had more to do with wanting to be close to her, rather than actually thinking he needed help, but he knew within minutes of arriving that his life was going to be so much easier here. With no stairs, and with Laura on hand and willing to help, he might

117

even have the opportunity to enjoy the babysitting experience.

And he especially enjoyed that Laura seemed to be relishing in her role of auntie. She looked so at home with the baby in her arms. He wanted to bring up the subject of their own situation so many times, to see if there was any way back for them, but the time was never quite right. Besides, he was worried about frightening her away again.

With the baby taking a nap, Laura at work, and a cup of tea and a biscuit waiting to be consumed, he switched the TV on and tuned into the world news channel.

The crew was in Bolivia.

He turned up the volume so he didn't miss a word. They were at the mine. Contact had been made.

'All twenty-two men trapped underground are reported to be safe and well.'

He let out a breath he hadn't realised he'd been holding. Matthew would be one of them. His brother-in-law was safe, although there would still be a long way to go to free the trapped men.

'They are surviving in an air pocket and have been sharing what food they have — packed lunches that have been pooled and rationed.

'Fresh supplies have been passed down to them through an initial bore hole. It is hoped that this may be widened to allow the miners to be freed but this may take some time.'

The cameras cut to the waiting crowd, picking out one anxious face he recognised. He sat up and leaned closer.

'I'm just so happy.' Kim was unable to hide her tears. 'We'd all feared the worse, but this is just the best news.' Fraser grinned. His sister, the master of understatement.

'I can't wait to see my husband again,' she continued, 'and to take him home.'

'Do you have any indication when that might be?'

Kim's sigh was heavy.

'It might take weeks. But as long as he's OK, that's all that matters.'

This was the first he'd seen or heard

of Kim for days. When she'd first arrived at the remotely located mine, she'd used the office landline to ring him and let him know she was OK. There was no mobile signal. She'd warned she might not be able to phone again for a while.

'Did you hear the news?' he asked Laura as soon as she walked in through the door. 'Matthew's all right.'

'Oh, that's wonderful,' she said, all smiles. 'When will they be home?' she added, a little more soberly.

'Not for a while, I expect. They made contact, but they still need to dig the men out.'

'You expect? Kim didn't say?'

'I didn't speak to her. I saw her on the news.'

'So we have Grace a little longer.'

'Looks like it.'

She smiled, obviously happy with the prospect of continued babysitting. But there was no getting away from the truth that his and Laura's time of playing happy families would soon be at an end.

'Go and wash your hands,' he told her,

forcing the depressing thoughts away. 'I'll have dinner on the table in five minutes.'

For now he was able to enjoy domestic bliss with the woman he loved, even if a lifetime together was out of the question.

And sometimes people had to make do and be content with snatches of borrowed happiness.

* * *

Grace was crying again. Laura heard the sounds from far away as they dragged her from her deep slumber. As she became alert, she could hear the quiet murmurings as Fraser tried to soothe the baby. and a soft lullaby that should have lulled the child back to sleep, but only served to make her howl even louder.

Bleary-eyed, she reached for her phone and checked the time. Four a.m. She wondered if Fraser had managed to get any sleep. She knew he'd still been up and awake, watching a film on TV when she had gone to bed shortly after midnight. She hadn't heard him turn in.

He had to still be in pain as his broken bone healed. Being awake half the night with a screaming infant would not be helping his recovery.

She hoped the baby would settle soon. But it seemed Grace would not be placated whatever Fraser seemed to do. The baby's howls cut through the dark and tugged straight at her heart.

She would have to be a robot to remain untouched by such misery. The wee soul, missing her mother and distressed beyond measure, was far more important than any notion Laura might have had about staying detached.

It went against everything she knew to be wise — but, so what, she asked herself, if she grew closer to Grace than she ought?

It wasn't as though she wasn't already completely and hopelessly in love with Fraser's tiny niece.

She got out of bed. Still in her nightshirt and with her feet bare, she left the safety of her bedroom and entered the pandemonium that had become her living-room.

Fraser seemed completely out of his depth, a look of utter bewilderment on his face as he paced the floor, his injured ankle hampering his progress, and the baby held with strong arms against his shoulder.

'I don't know what's wrong,' he said when he saw Laura, his tone apologetic. 'She's clean, dry, and fed. And she's been awake for the best part of the past twenty-four hours, so why isn't she tired?'

Laura didn't know.

'Maybe she's teething.' She plucked the suggestion out of a memory of Flora's girls at that age. She'd babysat them overnight once — and had realised then the exact meaning of double trouble. The memory still had the power to reduce her to a quivering wreck.

It had been terrifying. And she knew exactly how helpless Fraser would be feeling just now.

At the sound of her voice, the baby

123

turned her head towards the doorway and smiled as she saw Laura. She was all gums, with tears still wet on her cheeks.

Laura's heart contracted. Such a brave smile in the face of such determined heartbreak.

'What's all this about?' she asked in a soothing tone, instinctively stepping further into the room and reaching out to take the baby from Fraser's arms.

Grace brightened up at once.

'Maybe she just wants to be sociable. She probably thinks there's less chance of me trying to make her sleep.' Given that Laura had resolutely avoided bedtimes as well as nocturnal disturbances that wasn't an unreasonable supposition. Grace would associate Laura with fun and laughing and playtime.

And Laura didn't mind that one single bit.

Fraser made a sound that might have been exasperation.

'I'm obviously lacking the magic touch.'

She sent a sympathetic smile winging his way.

'You look exhausted. Go and grab some sleep. I'll take over this shift.'

He brightened up.

'You sure?'

She nodded. And she knew she'd made the right decision when Fraser's smile practically knocked her sideways, before he took her up on the offer.

'Shall we see what Mummy's put in the bag for you to play with?' she asked, as Grace rested her head on Laura's shoulder. The child had obviously tired herself out with her crying earlier. She suspected it wouldn't take much for the baby to nod off.

She found a couple of books in Grace's bag, and quickly selected one about a magic sheep named Trevor who travelled the world spreading happiness and doing good works. She recognised it as a favourite from when Flora's girls had been small. She knew the words had a gentle, lilting rhythm, and would be perfect to lull a little girl off to the land of nod.

'The Magical Land Of The Travelling Sheep.' She read the title in a soothing tone, settled Grace in her arms, and opened the cover to reveal the first glimpse of the colourful Trevor.

Laura glanced down fondly at the baby and, as she watched, Grace's eyelids grew heavy. The baby, despite her best efforts to fight against sleep, was powerless to resist the combination of soothing story and tiring day. Before long, her lids fluttered closed and Laura could tell from her breathing that the child was fast asleep.

Not wanting to disturb the baby when she'd finally settled, Grace settled herself on the sofa and leaned back against the cushions. She stifled a yawn, knowing she would have to take Grace through to her cot soon, but she was so cosy and comfortable, and the baby felt so right in her arms.

She would only close her eyes for a minute. Just until she was sure Grace was properly settled ...

* * *

It was two hours later that Fraser woke in a panic. The house was too quiet. Grace hadn't cried for ages.

He sat bolt upright, heart racing and glanced into the travel cot. She wasn't there. Then he remembered and relaxed. She would be with Laura.

He found them on the couch — the picture of serenity with Laura fast asleep, lying back against the cushions with Grace in her arms. He paused for a moment to take in the scene.

Laura was so beautiful, even asleep with no make-up and her hair messy. But it was more than that. Staying here with her had brought him peace in a way that had eluded him since she'd left. He felt he was truly at home.

As he watched, she opened one eye.

'I'm not asleep.'

He grinned. She made it sound as though sleeping would display some kind of weakness.

'I didn't say you were.'

'I didn't want to disturb Grace by putting her down.'

'It can't be comfortable there for you. I'll take her to her cot and you can go for a lie down.'

He scooped his sleeping niece into his arms, being careful not to wake her.

'It's probably time I got up in any case.' She stifled a yawn.

'Don't you have a day off today?'

She nodded.

'Then there's no hurry. Go back to bed and I'll bring you in a cup of tea after I've settled Grace.'

He was no more than five minutes, but by the time he took the tea to Laura, she was fast asleep, the covers pulled tightly around her like a cocoon.

So much for her talk of getting up. He smiled. Even if she hadn't complained, no doubt she'd suffered disturbed nights since he and Grace had arrived. For such a tiny thing, Grace certainly managed to make a lot of noise.

Quietly, he put the mug down on the bedside table. He wasn't about to wake

128

her, but she might be grateful for it if she stirred any time soon.

Then he took his own tea back to his own bed. No point in being the only one up when the house was so quiet. Best to rest when the baby was resting, in any case. At least that was what he recalled Kim saying.

Family Day

'I thought we could go out today,' Laura said as she refilled his coffee mug after brunch. 'Maybe take Grace to the park. You could both do with some fresh air, I'm sure.'

Laura drove them. It wasn't far, but she had insisted — and he knew she was right. With his ankle still giving him some problems, the distance he could walk was pretty limited.

As parks went, this wasn't the biggest. And he was lucky the paths were relatively smooth and devoid of any major inclines. The noise of children playing assaulted their eardrums long before they got near the play area.

'Sounds busy,' he said.

'It's always busy when the sun's out.' Her words were spoken with the assurance of an aunt who made frequent visits with her adored nieces.

It didn't look as though there were any spare benches in this part of the park.

130

He wondered if he should suggest going back — he needed to take the weight off his injured ankle. Despite the painkillers, it was beginning to throb.

'Laura, Fraser, over here,' a familiar voice called to them and he turned to find Flora sitting nearby. She shifted along to make room for both Laura and Fraser, and they sat down beside her.

Fraser couldn't hide his gratitude.

'Thanks.' He grinned.

He couldn't believe how tiring carting around his cast was turning out to be. He was fit. He'd always been physically active. He couldn't believe his body was letting him down like this when he'd always taken such good care of it.

'Where are the girls?' Laura asked as she unbuckled Grace from her pushchair and took her out to sit on her lap.

'Over there.' Flora pointed, and Fraser was slightly taken aback to see the girls on adjoining swings, with none other than Angus Irvine pushing first one and then the other.

'Angus was out for a run. We saw him

131

when we arrived. The girls were complaining that I never push them on the swings and he offered to step in.'

Fraser exchanged a quick glance of surprise with Laura, but neither made a comment. Flora's garbled explanation suggested she was self-conscious enough about the arrangement without either of them drawing attention to it.

Grace, right on cue to distract attention, began to gurgle and coo, taking in everything around her with wide eyes.

'Hopefully she'll sleep tonight if we can tire her out with fresh air and lots of things to look at,' Laura joked.

Flora was immediately sympathetic.

'Has she been keeping you awake at night? I remember before the twins were born people used to make jokes about sleepless nights and I used to think they were talking nonsense. But it really is no joke.'

'We're just about coping,' Fraser said with a grin. On his own, he knew he'd be struggling — he had no doubt about that. But with Laura by his side, anything was possible.

'It doesn't last long, though,' she said, glancing over at her girls. 'They grow up too quickly.'

As they all watched, the girls jumped from the swings and ran over to join the queue for the slide. There was no mistaking Angus's relieved expression as he came over to sit on the grass in front of the bench they were sharing.

'I'm worn out.'

'From pushing two small children on a couple of swings?' Fraser teased.

'You've no idea, mate. That was tougher than an hour's workout at the gym.'

Fraser doubted it, but he just smiled. It was nice to see his normally commitment-shy friend trying to impress a woman.

And there was no doubt in his mind, after Angus's reaction to Flora at Laura's flat the other week, that impressing Flora had been at the root of his sudden involvement in the Sunday morning play park culture.

'I think I'll take Grace to look at the ducks,' Laura said, getting to her feet and lifting the baby into an upright position against her shoulder. 'Can you keep an eye on the buggy?'

'Sure,' Flora said.

Fraser watched Laura walk towards the duck pond, which was over on the other side of the park to the enclosed play area and felt a sudden urge to follow her. It was daft — for the past two years he'd learned to live without her, but now he didn't want to be without her for a minute.

It was going to be tough when Kim came home. He'd have no excuse then not to move back to his own place. He was going to miss both of them — Laura and Grace. Which was very strange because he'd never had any particularly urgent thoughts about having children.

Grabbing his crutches, he got to his feet.

'I think I'll go with them,' he told the other two. 'Need the exercise.' And his throbbing ankle would just have to cope.

If they thought it odd, Angus and Flora didn't betray the fact by a single word or gesture. But that might be because they were too busy in conversation with each other to notice what he and Laura might be getting up to.

'They seem to be getting on well,' Fraser said as he reached Laura. He indicated back behind him with his head. 'Angus and Flora.'

'Angus is nice.' Laura bent down so Grace could get a closer look at the birds. The baby obligingly gurgled. 'These are ducks,' she supplied. 'One duck,' she pointed to one. 'Two ducks, three ducks, four. . .'

'Do you think Flora would be interested in a relationship?'

She straightened up and met his gaze.

'I don't know,' she told him honestly. 'We'd all like to see her settled again, but she went through such a difficult time when Lewis died. . .' She sighed.

'If Angus is wasting his time we should tell him.'

'Do you think he'd listen?'

Did Fraser himself listen when people warned him not to harbour hopes of Laura? Of course he didn't. And the more people — or Kim, to be exact — warned him off, the more he wanted to prove them wrong. 'I don't suppose he would.'

'That's what I thought.' She smiled, not unkindly. 'So maybe,' she continued, her tone gentle, 'just maybe, we should leave them to it and not interfere.'

He nodded. He didn't want to see his friend getting hurt, but this was really none of his business. Angus was a grown man — a tough firefighter — and he was well able to look out for himself.

He put the matter out of his mind when he spotted Flora pushing the empty buggy towards the pond, the twins scampering around behind, and Angus in his jogging gear looking like he belonged with this family.

It showed how appearances could be deceptive. But then to the outside world, he and Laura and Grace could pass for everyone's idea of a happy family.

'We were going back to my place for lunch,' Flora said. 'Would you three like to join us? It won't be anything special, just whatever I find in the freezer.'

'Sounds good,' Fraser said and Laura nodded.

It was as Flora was preparing the pizza and salad that they were having for Sunday lunch that she mentioned her daughters' upcoming birthday party.

'I hope you can still come,' she said anxiously to Laura.

'Try and stop me.'

'Fraser and Grace will be more than welcome, too.'

'Thanks,' Fraser said. His sister might be home with his brother-in-law by then but if not he knew his tiny niece would love it. He looked over to where she was asleep in her pushchair.

Already she could differentiate between adults and children and she had taken to Flora's girls. She'd giggled and gurgled at them when they'd been in the park — to such an extent that she was now exhausted.

Flora glanced towards the window to make sure her daughters were safely out of earshot and smiled as she saw them playing in the garden.

'I've booked a clown as a surprise,' she said, 'and a petting zoo. They bring the animals to you and let the children meet them. It's going to be pandemonium.'

For someone who was anticipating that level of chaos, Flora looked remarkably cheerful.

'Whatever happened to jelly and ice-cream and pass the parcel?' Angus asked with a laugh.

Flora sighed again.

'That's what I'd planned, but then the girls started asking if they could have a big party. I'll need all the help I can get.'

'Well, I'll definitely be here,' Laura promised. 'And I'm pretty sure you can add Mum and Dad to your list.'

'Count me in, too,' Angus said.

Fraser didn't miss the grateful smile Laura gave Angus as she brought plates and cutlery over to the table.

'Well, I'd love to be here,' Fraser said.

'But I don't know how much help I'd be with this.' He lifted his cast covered ankle.

'We'll get you a special chair,' Flora promised. 'And a whistle. You can be in charge of keeping order and making sure everyone hears the instructions.'

'I like the sound of that.' He grinned.

In practice he had no idea how it would turn out or how useful he would be, but at least Laura's sister was making room for him at this party.

* * *

'You don't have to come, you know. To the twins' party.' Laura felt she had to set the record straight as she drove them back to her place. 'If you'd rather not, nobody would blame you. After all, you are their aunt's ex-husband, so it's not really fair to expect you to help.'

He was quiet for a moment.

'Would you prefer I didn't go?' he asked eventually.

Yes, she would prefer that. It would

make life a lot neater and avoid a lot of complications. They'd had a good time today, just being normal and spending time with family — it would be too easy to slip into days like these and accept them as normal.

But it wasn't normal, and it couldn't last.

Laura felt a brief pang of sadness at the thought of Grace going. It was ridiculous, she had done all she could to keep herself safe from this and she had still fallen for Grace — and for her ex-husband.

Though, to be fair, she hadn't ever really fallen out of love with him. Just because all they had done when they'd lived together was to argue didn't mean she didn't love him.

'I have an interview,' she said, out of the blue, needing a diversion, but probably picking the only subject on earth that would be more stressful. 'For one of the jobs I applied for.'

As she kept her eyes on the road, she could practically hear his head snap around as he took in the news.

'Where is it?'

'London.' Just one word — but it signified that she'd be a world apart when she went — if she got this job.

'When?'

'Next Friday.' The day before her nieces' birthday party. Not wanting to leave Fraser on his own too long in his current situation, she was planning to fly down for the day.

'I didn't really believe you'd go.'

She stopped at a red light and risked a glance at him. His jaw was clenched — something that only ever happened when he was stressed and trying to control what he was saying.

Suddenly she didn't want him to be so controlled. She wanted him to make a fuss, to say all the things that would convince her to stay, even though she knew that if he said them, the best thing for both of them was still that she went.

'If you want to know the truth, I didn't think I'd really go, either.'

'But you will?'

The lights changed to green, and she returned her concentration to the road. 'If I'm offered the job, then yes — I will.' Because, really, what choice was there?

Party Time

Two very important men in her world — Fraser and Glenn — were both unhappy about her proposed move. Laura herself was also unhappy — and she didn't dare even think of how her family would react when she told them.

The interview had gone well. She was positive and fearful in equal measures. They had promised they would phone her when they had reached a decision.

While she was away, even though it had been just for the day, she had missed Fraser and Grace more than she'd thought. So much for the fact she had thought she'd put measures in place to protect her heart …

It was late when she arrived home, and her flat was quiet, though there was a light in the hallway to welcome her home. She dropped her bag on to the hall table and, before even taking off her coat, she tiptoed into the second bedroom. Fraser wasn't there, but Grace was fast asleep in her cot. The baby stirred in her sleep, and instinctively Laura reached out to stroke the baby's forehead and soothe her back to sleep.

She found Fraser in the living-room, sprawled over the sofa, also fast asleep — with the television flickering silently in the corner. Smiling, Laura turned the TV off, then picked a rug off the back of her chair and gently tucked it around him.

She worried that he wasn't as comfortable as he looked. Should she wake him? He stirred before she could decide.

'How did the interview go?'

'They're going to let me know next week.' She smiled. 'You waited up for me?'

'Of course I did.' He sat up, his eyes meeting hers and holding her gaze.

Her heart melted. She was so going to miss him not being here when she arrived home.

'Have you eaten?' he asked.

She nodded.

'I had something on the flight home.'

She glanced at her watch.

'It's nearly midnight. Time we both turned in if we're going to be bright and alert for the twins' party tomorrow.'

★ ★ ★

Laura was up early the next day, but Fraser and Grace were already in the kitchen. 'Someone was hungry,' he offered by way of explanation.

That much was evident from the way the spoonfuls of cereal he offered were eagerly received.

Laura laughed.

'She's a growing girl.'

Grace waved a chubby hand in the air and Laura went over and gave the baby a high five.

'And she'll need all her energy for the twins' party. There will be a lot for her to take in.'

Fraser nodded, then offered another spoonful of cereal to his baby niece. Then he looked up and the shock of his eyes looking directly into hers rendered her breathless.

He held her gaze for a moment longer than necessary, until Grace offered a loud squawk of objection that her breakfast had stopped coming. He quickly turned his attention back to feeding the baby.

'Kim phoned yesterday afternoon,' he told her. 'They hope to start bringing the workers up from the mine in the next few days.'

'That's great news,' Laura said. And it was — even if it meant Fraser and Grace would soon be leaving.

* * *

Fraser was amazed by just how much noise children were capable of making. Nothing in his previous, admittedly limited, experience had prepared him for the decibel level he was subjected to at Laura's nieces' party.

Laura laughed when she saw his face.

'It's what they do,' she said. 'Children. They make noise. It won't be long before this one's just as bad.' She nod-

146

ded towards Grace, who was settled in her arms.

He smiled.

'Grace makes enough noise already for such a wee thing.'

Before they knew it, they were all in the thick of the party — joining in, when encouraged to do so, with the magician's tricks. Grace took it all in, her large eyes darting around after the older children. And the whole time Laura didn't put her down once.

She suited a baby in her arms. She looked at home and utterly beautiful as she smiled at the baby.

He wondered, not for the first time, if things might have been different if they'd had a baby. Would they still be married?

He liked to think they would be. He allowed himself the brief fantasy for only a moment.

She must have sensed his gaze on her because she looked over and, when she smiled at him, he felt the breath whoosh from his lungs.

It was an intensely emotional moment.

And for that moment only the two of them existed — never mind the 30 children, or the magician, or the assorted adults who surrounded them. Or even the baby in her arms.

There was no way he was ever getting over her. No matter how far away from Tighnamor she went.

And Fraser knew he had to try to convince her to stay. Not to accept the job she might be offered that would take her so far away from her friends and her family — and from him. All the people who loved her.

The magician was approaching her now, drawn to her as most people were. He conjured a bunch of magical paper flowers into his hand. Fraser was pretty sure they had been stored up the man's sleeve, but like everyone else, he applauded.

'For you,' he said as he handed them to Laura.

Her smile was one of genuine delight.

'Thank you,' she said as she took one hand from Grace and accepted the gift.

'But I think maybe my sister, as hostess, should be the recipient.'

He smiled — that was typical Laura. She spent her life worrying that someone might be hurt or offended.

But Flora was laughing, obviously not offended in the least.

'Don't be silly,' Flora said. 'You've obviously inspired him.'

But it seemed the magician had another trick up his sleeve and instantly produced a second bouquet for Flora.

'Your boyfriend seems to have all bases covered,' Fraser teased Laura when he managed to get closer to her. 'You'd better watch out or he'll be asking for a date next.'

She laughed.

'He's not my type.'

'Are you sure? You seem to be his.' He was only teasing, but he was pleased to hear her vehement denial.

'Not jealous, are you?' She leaned towards him and lowered her voice. 'I have it on good authority that our magician has been happily married for the past forty years.'

Her tone was light, but her teasing about his being jealous hit home. He wasn't jealous of the older man in the slightest, but Laura was a young woman and, one day, she was bound to meet someone who was her type. Someone who would make her happy — who would chase the sadness from her eyes and ensure those lips were always smiling.

All he wanted was for her to be content. And if that was without him, then he would have to accept that.

But he didn't have to like it.

And he still didn't want her to leave Tighnamor.

How he wished he was the man who could make her happy.

★ ★ ★

'What does Fraser think he's doing?' Flora was standing next to Laura, her face a picture of disapproval.

Laura suspected she knew exactly the

thoughts going through Flora's head. Her sister would be wondering on what planet Fraser thought it might be a good idea to play football with a bunch of rowdy children getting in the way of his broken ankle and his crutches.

Laura could barely believe it herself. She was pretty sure that what he was doing could only result in tears. She winced as he gave the ball a mighty wallop with one of his crutches.

'I'm sure he knows what he's doing,' Laura said, sure of nothing of the sort, but feeling the need to speak up for her exhusband. She would feel disloyal doing anything else, even if Flora was her sister.

'Girls, I think one of you should tell Fraser to stop running around like that.' Nancy Robertson added her opinion to the conversation. 'I mean, it's one thing your father and Angus to be playing football, but neither of them is in plaster.'

'Fraser's fine, Mum. He's a big boy. He can look out for himself.' Laura only hoped her optimism wasn't misplaced.

Surely Fraser would be fine. Surely he couldn't be unlucky enough to injure himself twice in quick succession.

With baby Grace on her hip, she got up and began the task of one-handed tidying up, picking up plates and half-finished juice cups and stacking them carefully.

And she tried to ignore the niggling worry that, as a professional, she should warn Fraser to take it easy.

A loud commotion warned her something was wrong.

She turned to find Fraser sprawled on the ground, a number of small children seeming to have landed straight on top of him.

Her rescuer instincts kicked straight in and she'd handed the baby to Nancy before racing over to see if he was OK.

'I'm fine, I'm fine,' he confirmed as the children ran off in all directions, laughing as they went. 'What happened?' she asked as she knelt beside him.

He frowned.

'I'm not entirely sure.'

'Occupational hazard of playing football with small human beings.' Laura assumed her professional calm veneer, even though her heart raced. Fraser could have done himself a permanent injury. She should have listened to her mum and her sister and insisted he sit out the game of football.

'They have a tendency to get under the feet when they're in an excited crowd.'

He smiled — and a moment of intense intimacy was instantly created in the midst of the mayhem.

'I should have been more careful.'

'Are you hurt? Can you get up?'

He looked a little embarrassed.

'You're not going to believe this. . .'

'What?'

'I think I may have hurt my good ankle.'

'Oh.'

She was removing his shoe and sock so she could have a look at the offending ankle when Angus joined them.

'Problem?'

'He's hurt his good ankle.'

'Oh.'

'That's what she said.' Fraser made an attempt at humour and Laura smiled weakly, not finding the situation funny in the slightest. 'It'll be fine. I'll put some frozen peas on it.'

The echo of the night he'd ended up in plaster had Laura on high alert. The ankle was red and swollen. Fraser was downplaying the injury.

She bit back an angry retort — why had he put himself in this situation?

'I think we need to get this x-rayed.' She offered her professional advice.

'I'm fine,' he repeated. There was a circle of people around them now. Flora and Nancy had joined the group — as had Laura's dad, Drew Robertson.

'If Laura says you need to get it checked out, then you'd best do that, lad,' her dad said now.

She cast him a grateful glance. Her dad had always been immensely proud of her work and she was pleased he was supporting opinion now.

'You can drive him, Laura,' Nancy added. 'We'll look after Grace.'

Laura's heart swelled with love for her family that they were here now, offering moral support and practical help. Legally, Fraser was nothing to them now — and to most people an ex-son-in-law would be persona non grata.

But her lovely family had taken him into their hearts the day she'd married him, and they weren't about to let him go on a technicality.

She was going to miss these people so much when she left Tighnamor.

'Come on, tough guy,' she said, her jokey tone she hoped disguising the swell of emotion that was bubbling beneath the surface. 'Let's get you checked out.'

'How can I refuse an offer so beautifully put?'

Angus helped her to get Fraser to his feet and, after they'd both given Grace a quick kiss goodbye, they left the baby in the care of Laura's mother.

'Everything she needs is in her bag,' she told Nancy. 'Spare nappies, food, changes of clothes. . .'

'She'll be fine,' Nancy said. 'I do know

how to look after a baby, you know — I've raised two of my own. Take Fraser to hospital and get him checked out. The sooner you do, the sooner we'll know if he's fine and the sooner you'll be back.'

'I'm honestly fine,' Fraser insisted, even though it was blatantly obvious he was not.

'Don't be an idiot, Fraser. Ignoring it won't make the injury go away. Particularly not if you've managed a full set of broken ankles.'

In the end, Angus helped propel him into the passenger seat, while Laura devoted herself to the business of tucking his feet into the footwell and securing his seatbelt.

'I can do that myself,' he told her, his breath warm on her face as he spoke.

'Maybe you can, but you weren't doing it.' Her words were light and playful, but really she just wanted to get him checked out and arguing over the seatbelt was the last thing on her agenda.

They drove along for a few minutes, neither of them speaking. She wondered if he, too, was thinking that their days playing at happy families with baby Grace were numbered.

'The lengths I have to go to so you'll agree to go on a date with me.' Fraser was the first to break the silence.

Despite the jokey remark, there was an undertone of tension to his words. Laura glanced quickly across and saw that he was looking very pale.

'You OK?'

'I'll live.'

'I'm pleased to hear it.' But she was worried about him. It was obvious he was in pain and she didn't know how he would cope with another broken ankle. Surely he wouldn't be that unlucky, she hoped for the second time.

It didn't take them long to get to A&E.

'Stay here,' she told him as she got out from behind the wheel.

'What for?'

But she smiled and declined to answer. She knew he wouldn't be happy and there was no point in starting the argument any sooner than she needed to.

She was back with her prize within moments and, predictably, he objected.

'You've got to be kidding.' His eyes held a steely resolve as she opened the passenger door and presented him with the only alternative they really had. 'I don't need a wheelchair.'

'I'm afraid you do.' She didn't mind doing her share of the lifting and carrying in her daily work, but there were limits. Her concerned brown eyes took in all six foot four inches of pure muscle. 'There's no way I can take your weight on my own. Angus had to help you into the car, remember?'

Grudgingly he allowed himself to be helped into the hospital.

'We're busy today,' the triage nurse told them. 'It may be a long wait.'

'Has something happened?' Laura knew that any Saturday night was likely to be busy in A&E, but it was only late afternoon. The DIY brigade would have been dealt with and it was too early for the party mob.

'Pile up on the motorway outside

town,' he explained. 'There are a couple of nasty injuries as well as some walking wounded. They're all in shock. We'll get to you as soon as we can.' The last comment was directed to Fraser, who nodded.

'No hurry. We've all the time in the world.'

Laura wished that were true. Time was ticking away for them. Soon, Grace's parents would arrive back to claim her, Fraser would leave Laura's flat and return to his own house, and eventually Laura would leave Tighnamor.

For now, though, she had a duty to do her best for him. He may be her ex-husband, but he was still the love of her life.

'I'll get us some tea,' she told him, parking his chair in front of the large screen TV that was showing some 24-hour news channel. Presumably her suggestion met with his approval, because he didn't even attempt to argue.

'Thanks.' He took the paper cup that was full of some nondescript liquid from the vending machine, his gaze fixed on the screen.

She glanced over to the screen, shock numbing her legs, so she dropped on to the plastic seat beside Fraser.

'They're in Bolivia,' she stated as realisation dawned. 'Is that Matthew's mine?'

Fraser didn't turn from the screen. His weary objections and irritation at his new injury were forgotten and replaced by absolute concentration on the news.

'I think so.'

The sound was off, but the subtitles made clear what was going on.

'They're bringing the men up,' Laura said unnecessarily — Fraser was as capable as she was of reading the words on the screen.

She reached out and her hand met his — his fingers curling around hers and holding them tightly. She felt safe when he held her hand — despite the uncertainty that still plagued them over the fate of his brother-in-law.

They both knew without needing to be told that the operation to bring the men up was risky. They wouldn't be able to relax until Matthew and his colleagues were on the surface.

'They'll be home soon,' she said, pleased by the conviction she could hear in her own voice. 'Kim and Matthew. We have to believe that.'

He nodded — and absently raised her fingers to his lips and brushed the lightest of kisses along the back of her hand.

That was something he'd done all the time when they'd been married.

Now that they were no longer man and wife she knew it was no longer appropriate. But she found that she couldn't object. She needed the reassurances of those kisses every bit as much as he needed to offer them.

* * *

The ankle was only bruised.

'I feel an idiot.' Fraser fastened his seatbelt and they prepared to drive back to Flora's house to collect Grace.

'You'd have felt even more of an idiot if it had been broken and we'd done

161

nothing about it.'

'I should have known. It didn't feel anything like the other one when that went.'

Laura smiled as she put the car into gear.

'You did say you would be fine with a bag of frozen peas with the broken one,' she reminded him. 'It was the rest of us who insisted on you getting it checked out.'

She smiled, fully recognising the embarrassment he must be experiencing. As emergency workers, they all had the same fear of wasting the time of medical professionals. Their mantra with their own injuries was always to wait and see how things were the next day.

But on the night of his first accident, he'd been overruled by paramedics on site. And today, with one broken ankle already, Fraser hadn't been allowed the luxury of waiting.

'Maybe next time you'll take a bit more care of yourself.'

'I was pushed,' he argued. 'Those

children might be small, but they're complete menaces.'

She smiled. He wasn't wrong. There was nothing quite as scary as a group of excited children. She turned the ignition key.

'I'm glad we got you checked out. We were worried about you.' He found it impossible to look away from her face as she manoeuvred the car out of the car park.

'I was worried about you.'

Had she really just said that? Fraser's eyes narrowed as he tried to read her expression. He took in her profile — there wasn't even a trace of humour. And it meant more than he could ever admit that she'd made that confession.

Not that he wanted her to worry about him, but it was good to know she cared. Especially as, if all went to plan, Grace's parents would be home soon. And then all he and Laura would have left would be whatever feelings still remained for each other.

Over the time they'd been caring for Grace, Laura and he had grown closer. They had been like a family.

Without Grace, they would revert to being two people who had once been married. Unless he could persuade her to stay here with him in Tighnamor.

His heart skipped a beat at the thought. If he'd had a good foot left he would have kicked himself for ever letting her go in the first place.

They were only streets away from Flora's house when his mobile buzzed to life. He fished it from his pocket and glanced at the display.

'It's Kim.'

'Well, answer it,' she said impatiently.

Kim didn't keep him long. The news both elated him and brought him crashing down to the depths of despair.

'Matthew's safe,' he told Laura. The news item had only shown the first two workers rescued, neither of whom had been Matthew. 'They'll be home soon.'

'Thank goodness for that.' Her words

were heartfelt, but the light in her eyes died. He guessed her emotions were as conflicted as his own.

A First Date

'Tired?' Flora put a coffee down on her kitchen table in front of Laura.

'What gave you that idea?' Laura asked drily, as she stifled another yawn. It had been a tough shift. All she'd wanted was to get home to Fraser and Grace. She knew her make-believe family would not be together much longer and she wanted to make the most of every minute.

But then she'd read her sister's text, and there was no way she could ignore it. Flora hardly ever needed advice — this had to be serious. There was no way she could refuse Flora's request for a quick chat over coffee.

'Baby keeping you up?'

Laura nodded.

'You'll miss her when Kim's back.'

'I know.'

'But at least you'll be able to see her — spend time with her. Just like you do with the girls.'

There was no way Flora could know

that she was digging herself in deeper. No way she could know about the interview Laura still hadn't heard about — and the other jobs she'd applied for. If any of those materialised into an offer she would be hundreds of miles away. Amelia and Jessica and Grace would grow up not really knowing her. She'd be nothing more than an absent aunt.

But at least she would be able to keep in touch with Flora's girls from afar. There would be phone calls and video calls shared — there would be visits for holidays and birthdays.

Once Grace went back to her parents, once Fraser went home, once Laura herself moved away, there would be no reason to keep in touch.

She would never see Grace again. Her heart cracked a little.

She would probably never see Fraser again, either. She took a deep breath. The pain was almost unbearable.

'What did you want to talk to me about?' Laura asked. Not a very subtle way to change the subject, but it was the best she could do.

Flora put down her coffee cup and frowned.

'Angus has asked me out.' Flora's face was a picture of conflict. 'He wants me to go to dinner with him tomorrow night.'

'Fraser's friend Angus?'

'What other Angus would it be? He barely had chance to talk to me when he helped out at the girls' birthday party, but then I saw him when I nipped to the shop. He just blurted the question out.'

This had been the last thing Laura had expected. She didn't quite know what to say.

'What did you tell him?'

Flora's face reddened.

'That I'd think about it.'

At least it hadn't been an out and out refusal.

'I think you should say yes. You've been widowed two years now. It's time you dated again.'

Flora glanced at the wedding ring she still wore. She didn't say anything, but her feelings were obvious to a sister who knew her well and cared about her very much.

'He wouldn't want you to be on your own for the rest of your life,' Laura told Flora gently.

'I know. He said that — when he was ill. He made me promise I'd find someone who would be good to me and the girls. But I'd still feel disloyal. It just doesn't seem right. Like I'm being unfaithful to his memory.'

Laura looked sympathetic.

'I know. But you mustn't think like that. Angus wasn't proposing marriage, after all — just a date. And he's lovely. You might even have fun.'

'But the girls ... I can't leave them to go for a night out.' Flora was looking for excuses.

Laura was having none of it.

'The girls will be fine. I'll come over here and bring Fraser and Grace and we can make an evening of it.'

'Do you have Angus's number?' Laura knew that Fraser would have it, if not.

Flora nodded.

'He asked for my number and texted his to me when I said I needed time to think.'

'Phone him,' Laura urged. 'Tell him yes.'

* * *

Fraser glanced at the kitchen clock. Laura was late. He turned the oven down, to keep dinner warm. It seemed to act as a catalyst — only moments later she arrived home.

'Hey, should you be on your feet?' she asked him as she came into the kitchen and dropped a kiss on Grace's down-covered head as she sat in her highchair.

'I'm fine.' He waved his hand dismissively. 'Yesterday's injury is forgotten, and the broken ankle is much more comfortable. Dinner won't be long.'

Laura smiled.

When they'd been married, he'd often had dinner waiting for her when she'd arrived home. He'd enjoyed doing it

— preparing a meal with love, sitting with her as they ate and discussed their respective days.

The same thoughts seemed to be crossing her mind and she seemed to be resisting them. As he watched, her smile turned to a frown.

'Don't do that,' he told her gently.

'Do what?'

'Shut me out.'

'This is just too cosy.' She sighed. 'It's going to hurt too much when it all ends.'

He was at her side in seconds, reaching out to her, and she stepped willingly into his embrace. He held her tightly, never wanting to let her go.

The familiar scent of her shampoo teased his nose and she slipped her arms around his waist and held him back, though he didn't hold out any hope that this was progress. It was more an echo of what had once been.

'Any news from Kim?'

'I haven't heard anything since she told us that Matthew's in hospital, getting checked over. Hopefully they'll get a chance to ring when they know flight times.'

It seemed the most natural thing in the world that they should have this conversation, standing in the middle of the kitchen, still holding each other tightly.

'They had a tough time of it down that mine between lack of supplies, bad air quality, and such. It will be a while before he's fully back to peak condition.'

She nodded, and began to set the table for dinner as he found the oven gloves and took the casserole dish out.

It was as they ate dinner that she shared her own news. Fraser wasn't surprised that Angus had asked Flora out.

'I'm glad he finally found the courage.'

Laura nodded in agreement.

'And we're babysitting.'

He grinned — liking the idea of helping Laura take care of her nieces every bit as much as he liked that the fact that she was helping him to look after baby Grace.

* * *

Flora opened the door as soon as the car pulled up outside.

'Hi,' Laura called, stopping only to unstrap Grace's car seat before carrying the baby up the pathway.

Fraser followed carefully behind — more sure now on his crutches, but still wary after his football accident.

Flora was frowning as she led them all into the living-room. She was still dressed in the universal mum's uniform of jeans and T-shirt, and it seemed she'd made no move to get ready for her date.

'Where are the girls?' Laura put Grace, still sitting in her seat, down on the living-room rug.

'In bed.'

Laura lifted an eyebrow.

'Already?' She couldn't pretend she wasn't disappointed.

'It's a school night.' Flora threw herself on to the sofa.

Laura glanced at the clock on the mantelpiece.

'Er, Angus will be here soon. Don't you think you should be getting ready?'

173

'No — I think I should phone him to cancel.'

'Why do you think that?' Laura asked calmly.

'Well, the girls . . . I really don't think I should be leaving them . . . I've been so worried about doing the right thing. I mean, if it feels so wrong then perhaps it is.'

So there wasn't a concrete reason — nothing had happened, nothing had changed — it was merely cold feet on Flora's part.

'Oh, Flora.' Time for action. She took her sister's arm and swept her towards the stairs. 'Let's go and see what we can find for you to wear.'

Flora was scared witless — that much was obvious. She needed careful advice if she was to realise that her nerves were entirely natural in the circumstances.

'I don't know what I'm doing,' Flora admitted as Laura went through her wardrobe, considering and rejecting outfits one by one. 'I shouldn't be doing this. I have responsibilities.'

'And you always more than meet those responsibilities, but you're allowed a life, too.'

'But the girls ...'

'The girls will be fine for one evening. You're leaving them with responsible adults.' She selected a jersey dress in the softest blue — it was smart without being too dressy. She thrust it unceremoniously at her sister. 'Here, this will do. You always look lovely in it.'

Flora took the dress without argument and quickly put it on.

'Sit,' Laura instructed, pointing at the stool next to the dressing table. Quickly she applied a little mascara and lipstick ... Her sister didn't need much make-up — just a touch to give her a bit of confidence. A brush though her hair, a quick upsweep and a couple of pins to secure it in place, and Flora was ready.

The sound of male voices in the kitchen alerted them to the fact Angus had already arrived to pick Flora up.

'Fraser must have let him in,' Laura said unnecessarily.

'Ready?' Laura asked.

Flora took a deep breath, then gave a short nod.

'Ready,' she agreed.

★ ★ ★

'That was pretty traumatic,' Fraser commented after Flora and Angus had left for their night out and he and Laura were settling down in front of the TV — a sleepy Grace nestled in his arms. 'I thought she was going to cry off.'

'Me too,' Laura admitted. It seemed the most natural thing in the world for her to sit beside him and rest her head on his shoulder.

'I hope we've done the right thing,' he said. 'Pushing her into this. What if it all goes horribly wrong?'

Laura sat up. His expression gave nothing away.

'Do you think that's likely?'

'Honestly? No. I think they're very well suited. I think — if she lets him — he'll make her very happy. But there's always the possibility, isn't there, that things might go awry?'

'Yes.' She got the feeling he was no longer talking about Flora and Angus.

She leaned back — careful this time not to make contact with him, but she reached out to touch Grace's tiny fingers.

'Fraser?'

'Mmm?'

'If you'd known things would go so wrong for us, would you still have taken the chance?'

She could hear the blood rushing through her ears as she waited for his reply. If he said that he regretted their marriage, she didn't think she would be able to bear it. Even if ending it had been the sensible thing to do in the end.

'Yes,' he told her softly, as he reached out to her free hand. 'Every single time.'

She allowed his fingers to curl around hers and was comforted by his touch.

'Me too,' she finally admitted.

'But I don't know about Flora and Angus.' He frowned. 'Meddling with their relationship is none of our business. They have to be able to make their own mistakes — and maybe we should have let her cancel if that was how she felt.'

Laura hoped he was wrong. She hoped that all Flora had needed was encouragement and her hesitation hadn't been deeper rooted.

What if she really wasn't ready for a new relationship? It wasn't only Flora and Angus who might be hurt — Laura's nieces had to be considered here, too.

She got up and gently passed Grace into Fraser's arms.

'I'm going to check on the girls,' she told him and he gave a short nod.

They were both fast asleep in their identical twin beds — like two tiny angels. She tucked the pink quilts gently around them, then kissed each warm forehead.

Downstairs, she made tea, then joined Fraser in the living-room.

'Thanks.' He grinned as he took the mug from her.

There was a film on TV — a comedy, she gathered, from the occasional chuckle coming from Fraser. She couldn't concentrate, though. Not when she was worried about her sister.

When she heard the key in the front door, she was on her feet before Flora had even stepped off the doorstep.

'Well?'

Flora smiled.

'It was a good evening.'

It was only then, when she was able to finally relax, that Laura realised how tense she'd been. She smiled back.

'I mean, he's not Lewis, of course. If Lewis was still here. . .' She sighed, her eyes filled with sadness.

Laura put an arm around her sister's shoulder.

'I know.'

'But Lewis is gone,' Flora added softly. 'And I have to face the fact that he's never coming back.' She sighed. 'If things were the other way around, I wouldn't want him to be alone. I'd want him to meet someone else.'

'And you think that your someone else might be Angus?'

179

'I don't know.' She took off her jacket and hung it up on the coat stand. 'But I haven't ruled it out.'

Homecoming

'Are they going to see each other again?' Fraser asked Laura as they drove home. He'd been in the living-room when she and Laura had been talking in the hall-way — no doubt he would have heard their voices, but the TV would have drowned out what had been said.

'I hope so,' Laura said as she turned the car into her street.

Fraser didn't reply as she'd expected, but he sat forward in his seat.

'That looks like Kim's car.' He pointed towards the line of cars that had parked at the kerb outside Laura's flat. 'It is Kim's car. They're back.'

With those words, Laura had to face the fact that it was over. Her time with Grace and Fraser had finally come to an end.

As soon as the car stopped, Kim and Matthew came running over, Kim pulling open the back door and swooping down on Grace.

'Hello, my angel.' She kissed the baby before turning to the two sitting in the front. 'And hello to you, too.'

'Hey,' Fraser greeted her, while Laura smiled — how could she not when a baby and her parents had been reunited after such a stressful time? 'Why didn't you tell us you were on your way?'

'I tried to phone your mobile from the airport, but it kept going to answerphone.'

Fraser checked his phone and grimaced.

'It's off. Battery must have run down. Sorry.'

But Kim wasn't listening. She gently lifted Grace from her car seat, the baby cooing happily as she snuggled into her mother — Matthew putting his arms around his family and holding them tight.

'There were times,' he said when he eventually let them go, 'when I thought I wouldn't see these two again.'

'How did you get back so quickly?' Laura asked. It just didn't seem possible that they had arrived back already. 'I thought you were in hospital for observation?'

Matthew looked up.

'I convinced them I was fine so they let me go,' he said with a grin. 'And we were lucky with flights. I can barely believe we're back.'

'Do you want to come in?' Laura asked. It was late and she guessed they would be keen to get home, but she had to ask.

'Thank you,' Kim said, 'but I need to get those two home.'

Laura smiled — completely understanding. She would have been the same under similar circumstances.

'What about Grace's things?' Fraser asked.

'We'll get them in the morning,' Matthew said. 'We've enough at home to manage for tonight.'

'Thank you for taking care of her,' Kim said, smiling over the baby's head. 'Both of you. You can't know what a comfort it was for me to know she was in such safe hands.'

'It was a pleasure,' Laura said quietly, forcing a smile.

She was speaking for Fraser as well — as though they were still a married couple. But that was the least of her worries.

Kim glanced at Matthew and they exchanged a glance so sweet that Laura felt the warmth of tears in her eyes.

Laura and Fraser stood at the side of the road, watching the family drive off — both too shocked to move.

'I didn't think they'd be back so suddenly,' he said.

'Neither did I.' She'd thought she'd be fine with this — she really had. But now that it had happened, she really didn't know how to react.

She was aware of Fraser moving heavily on his crutches towards her as she stared into the empty road.

'Come on,' he said gently, taking her hand. 'Let's get indoors. It's getting late.'

She didn't want to go in. She knew the flat would be empty. Missing Grace would be all the more real. Especially with her highchair, cot, toys. . . all her things around them.

Too numb to argue, she allowed Fraser to lead the way inside.

'Sit there,' he told her, nodding towards the sofa. 'I'll make us some tea.'

On some level, she was aware he must be in pain — his old injury would be aching, no doubt, his fresh one still throbbing merrily. He showed no sign of it, though. He was being strong — exactly what she needed.

Her heart squeezed even tighter.

He brought the tea in awkwardly, on one crutch, one cup at a time.

★ ★ ★

Fraser had seen Laura like this once before. When they had decided to part.

Both in demanding jobs with conflicting schedules, they had barely seen each other. And when they had they had argued.

Flora's husband had been gravely ill

at the time, and Laura had moved out initially to help her sister look after her nieces.

She'd never come home.

He should never have let it become permanent. He should have tried harder to save their marriage.

He sat down beside her now, on the sofa, and she didn't even seem to register he was there.

'Drink up,' he urged when she didn't seem able to move. On some level, his words got through, and she looked down at the tea in her hand, frowning — almost as though she couldn't work out how it got there.

Gently, he reached out and guided the cup up towards her lips. He'd put plenty of sugar in it, and he guessed she needed that right now. She didn't resist. He didn't think she was capable of resisting. The liquid barely touched her lips, but she took a brief sip before putting the mug back down on the coffee table.

Two years ago, he hadn't realised what was at stake. Now he knew exactly what he would lose.

There was a chance for them. This time with Grace had proved that. All he had to do was convince her. Because if he didn't, Laura was going to walk out of his life — and maybe he wouldn't see her for another two years, possibly even longer, once she moved away from Tighnamor.

'She's gone.' Laura's voice was so quiet he had to lean towards her to make out the words. 'She's really gone.'

'We'll still see her.'

'I suppose we will.' But she didn't sound convinced.

Fraser wondered if he should offer to go back to his own place now. His reason for staying here was no longer valid — there would be no requirement for him to carry a baby up and down stairs with his ankle injury. But he didn't want to leave her. And it took only one look at her face to convince him she was in no state to be left on her own.

The tears, when they came, were a shock. Laura never cried. But now silent

trails of misery were working their way
down her face.

He moved closer, put an arm around
her and, as she rested her head on his
shoulder, he hugged her tight. He had
longed so much to hold her in his arms
again — but he hadn't wanted it to be
like this. Not with her so unhappy.

★ ★ ★

It was the early hours of the morning
before she managed to drag herself away
from Fraser's comforting hug.

'It's late,' she said, sitting up. 'We
should turn in.'

He gave a short nod.

'I'm sorry about earlier.' She sniffed.

He shrugged.

'Nothing to be sorry for.'

'I overreacted.'

'You didn't. It was a shock. If Kim had
let us know they'd be back so soon, we
could have prepared — been ready to let
her go.'

'I was never fussed about having a

baby around the house, but I fell in love with her.'

'Babies have a way of worming their way into our affections — it's nature, it's how they can be sure they'll be protected and looked after.'

She knew the biology, but the strength of her feelings for Grace — and in such a short time, too — had shocked her. She was a professional. It was her job to care. But she didn't fall to pieces every time she handed a patient over to A&E.

She wondered how it might be to have a baby of her own, but stopped herself from saying the words out loud.

'You're human,' he said, getting to his feet. 'You're caring and loving and don't beat yourself up about that.'

Her smile was genuine. This man was so lovely — she couldn't bear the fact that soon she would have to let him go, too. She was only grateful he hadn't already suggested leaving. Even if, in the years they'd been apart, she'd grown accustomed to living alone, she needed to know that there was someone else alive and breathing in the same flat tonight.

'I'll be all right in the morning.' She smiled again — more to convince herself that she meant what she said than anything else.

* * *

Fraser heard Laura get up and move around in the kitchen. He hadn't slept a wink — and it seemed neither had she.

It had been good to see Kim and Matthew home safely, but he still wished baby Grace could stay with him and Laura a little longer.

These past few weeks, despite the desperate worry for Matthew and the miners trapped so far below ground, had meant a lot. He and Laura had been getting along in a way that they hadn't since they'd first married.

He eventually managed to get on to his feet and put his dressing-gown on before going to join Laura in the kitchen.

She smiled when she saw him and he nearly stopped breathing.

'Hi. If I'd known you were awake I'd have brought you in a cuppa.'

Just like that, normality was restored and it was almost as though the heartache of Grace going back to her parents yesterday hadn't even happened.

He decided to take her lead.

'Can't have you waiting on me like that — you're not running a hotel.' He still accepted the cup of tea she brought over for him. 'Thanks.'

'Do you have plans for today?' She made the question sound casual, but he knew how much it must have cost her to gloss over the fact that he should have been looking after Grace.

'I might ring the station later. See if they can take me back.' Now his sister no longer needed his help, he would be bored out of his mind at home without anything to do.

'You can't do that.' She was appalled. 'You'd be a liability — not to mention putting yourself in danger.'

'They'll have stuff I can do at the station.'

She didn't look convinced.

'Well, as long as you make sure you don't go out on calls.'

He was pretty sure she was worrying about nothing. Health and safety rules were so strict he'd be lucky if they let him sit at a desk until he was deemed fit for active duty. But he had to try.

'Did you have anything planned for today?' he asked, wishing he didn't have to. He knew she'd probably been looking forward to spending today with Grace — mainly because that was what she'd been doing on her days off ever since he and Grace had come to stay with her.

'We could pack Grace's things up and take them over to Kim and Matthew. They'll have a lot to do today so that will save them a job.'

If he didn't know her so well, he might have missed the tremor in her voice. She was battling hard to keep things as normal as possible and he was so proud of her for doing so.

'Then maybe as it's a nice day, if you fancied,' she continued, 'we could take a drive into the country? Maybe stop off at a pub for lunch?'

Even if it hadn't been a nice day, even if it had been blowing a force ten gale and there was a blizzard, the idea of a day out with Laura was definitely something he fancied.

'OK.' He didn't want to read too much into this. He didn't want to frighten her by being too keen. These things had to be taken slowly and steadily.

Maybe she might want him without the baby after all.

His heartbeat went into overdrive at the prospect.

* * *

Laura didn't know where that invitation had come from. For a moment, she wished she could take it back. They'd already decided there was no future for them as a couple.

But the more she thought about it, the more a day out with Fraser made sense. They would both be missing Grace and spending the day together, as neither had other plans, was the sensible thing to do.

Kim was a lot less hostile than she had been on the few occasions that Laura had seen her since the divorce.

'Come in,' she said, her hair still messy, and her dressing-gown proof that she hadn't been up for long.

'I'm sorry,' Laura said. 'We really shouldn't have disturbed you this early.'

'I have a baby,' Kim said, casting Laura an amused glance. 'I've been up since six.'

Laura smiled.

'Of course.' How she wished she was still the one that Grace was waking at the crack of dawn.

Grace was in her highchair, waving a spoon about. She gave a gummy smile when she saw Laura and Fraser and Laura's heart squeezed tight in her chest. Without thinking, she went over and lifted Grace up for a cuddle. When she realised, she turned, horrified at how overly familiar she had been, to apologise.

'I'm so sorry,' she told Kim. 'I shouldn't have done that.' She went to put Grace back, but Kim came over and put a hand on her arm.

'I think you've more than earned the right to a cuddle when you see her, don't you?'

Laura could feel the sting of tears in her eyes, and could only nod.

'How's Matthew?' Fraser asked as he limped over to Laura and popped a quick kiss on the baby's head. Grace giggled and tried to reach out to pull his hair. He took the baby's hand.

'No you don't, madam.' He laughed. Then he turned to Kim. 'It's a game she likes.'

Kim sighed.

'I wasn't even away that long, but I seemed to have missed so much. She's changed already.' She sighed again. 'Matt's still asleep. The whole experience has taken it out of him.'

They declined Kim's offer of a cup of tea after Grace's things had been unloaded from Laura's car.

'We'll leave you to get on,' Fraser said. 'You've been through a lot, too.'

It was only at that point that Kim began to cry softly.

'Happy tears,' she insisted when they both fussed over her. 'I can't believe it's all over and my family is all at home together again.'

Kim soon regained her composure and Laura and Fraser left.

'Seems strange,' she said as they drove out of town, 'not to have to keep checking the car seat.'

'We'll get used to it,' he said.

They would. Not that she wanted to. But he seemed disinclined to keep talking about missing Grace, so she took the hint and tried to concentrate on their day out, instead.

They found a little tea room, out in the wilds, where they stopped for a sandwich lunch. It was overlooking a small loch, trees overhanging and hidden from the road. If they hadn't spotted a half-hidden sign on the main road they would have missed it completely.

'Would you like to sit out on the deck?' the man behind the counter asked. 'I'll bring your order out when it's ready.'

That wasn't an offer they were going to refuse. The view from the deck was breathtaking.

'I've lived nearby all my life, but I didn't even know this place was here,' Laura said. 'I could live in a place like this.'

'Me too,' he said. And she was grateful he didn't point out the irony of the fact she'd applied for a job in London — the exact opposite of this small, remote place.

She wondered if it might be an idea to bring up their living arrangements while they ate. Now Grace had gone, and especially now he was thinking he might try to go back to work in some capacity, was it appropriate for him to still stay at her place?

She couldn't bring herself to suggest he move out. By the time they were on their way she had made up her mind that maybe there might be a future for them

197

after all.

They'd been getting on so well.

★ ★ ★

By the time they arrived back at the flat Laura had realised how stupid it would be to let him go again. Fate had brought him back into her life for a reason.

All she had to do now was to find out if he felt the same way. Given he'd asked her not to leave Tighnamore, she suspected he might do.

He'd gone for a lie down to rest his painful ankles.

And, as though it was waiting for the moment she had made up her mind about her future, the phone began to ring.

It was news about the job she had applied for.

'We're pleased to offer you the post,' the chair of the interview panel told her.

The silence since her interview had lulled her into a false sense of security. She guessed it was the same with Fraser

— he hadn't mentioned her plans, either.

Now, however, they would be forced to face the fact that she would be starting a new life without him — leaving him free to start a new life without her.

It wasn't a prospect that filled her with joy.

Casualty

'So Fraser's still staying in your spare room?' Glenn waded right in with the interrogation as they waited for the next call.

There were no secrets in Tighnamor.

'It's easier with his ankle. There are too many stairs at his place.' The excuse sounded flimsy, but the truth was that neither of them had brought up the subject of him moving out.

'Have you told him about the job offer?'

'Not yet.'

'You're going to have to soon.'

'I know.'

'I mean, he's going to notice if you're suddenly just not there any more.'

'I know. Look, Glenn, you don't have to spell it out for me. I'm just waiting for the right time. I'll tell him when I'm ready.'

He frowned.

'You did accept it?'

It would be easier if she had, but faced with what she'd wished for only a few short weeks ago, she'd lost her nerve.

'I asked them for time to think.' She sighed. She suspected they must think she was an idiot. 'Can we not talk about this just now, please? I haven't even got my own head around it yet.'

Glenn was quiet again — seemingly having taken her at her word. She was glad. Not only did she not want to talk about it, she really didn't want to think about it either. There was no way she was ever getting her head around a life-changing move of this magnitude.

Once again she wished she hadn't confided in Glenn. But he was a good friend. The best. And she trusted him with her life. She spent more of her waking time with him than with anyone else.

And they had seen things together that human beings shouldn't have to see and as a team they'd worked to keep their broken patients together long enough to hand them over to the doctors who would attempt to repair any damage.

That kind of thing created a bond.

She'd owed him it to tell him. He would be affected by her decision, too. He would have to build up a new relationship with a new partner. It wasn't quite a divorce — but it was close. As close as it could be for two people who weren't related or romantically involved.

But there were still some things she didn't want to talk about at the moment. And leaving Tighnamor — and Fraser — was one of them.

'No problem. I get it,' he said, sounding resigned. 'I'll change the subject. How are things going with your sister and that fireman?'

That was better. It was none of her business to be discussing her sister's romance, but Flora and Angus had been seen out for dinner and going dancing — so she wouldn't be breaking any confidences if she told Glenn.

'Things seem to be going well.' They were actually going much better than Laura could have ever hoped for. It was very early days, but she suspected they might be falling in love. And she was glad. Her sister deserved to be happy.

'And have you told her that you're going to be moving?' He seemed unable to leave the subject alone.

'Not yet,' she replied, wondering what part of her assertion that she didn't wish to discuss this subject that Glenn had difficulty understanding.

'I wonder how she'll take it. You seem to be babysitting for her a lot these days.'

'She'll be fine. As long as I'm happy, she'll be happy. And Mum will jump at the chance of staying with the girls whenever Flora wants to go out. I've had to fight her off already.'

She hoped that would be an end to Glenn's inquisitiveness. There was really nothing to gain by talking about her move. She wondered how she could change the subject — permanently this time.

Glancing out through the windscreen into the dark sky beyond, Laura experienced a sickening sense of déjà vu as her wish seemed to be granted in a most unwelcome manner. There was an orange glow in the night sky.

'Look at that,' she told Glenn. 'It's over towards the industrial estate again.' She prepared the ambulance for a quick getaway. 'Another fire, do you think?'

'I hope not.'

But even as they watched, the glow intensified.

Glenn took the call a second later, his tone grave as he gave his response.

'They need us over there,' he confirmed.

'I don't like this.' Laura steered the ambulance along the deserted streets. 'Someone is going to get seriously hurt if they don't put a stop to whatever maniac is doing this.'

'We don't know yet that it's deliberate.'

'Coincidences don't happen in threes.'

She hated that someone might be maliciously endangering lives. She and Glenn and their colleagues spent their time trying to save people and knowing someone might deliberately be trying to cause harm went against everything she believed in.

'It just makes me so cross that anyone could. . .' Even speaking about the unknown fire-raiser brought up so much emotion she wasn't able to finish her sentence.

'I know.' Glenn's voice was resigned. 'Me too.'

And she knew that any one of her colleagues would have understood.

She also knew as soon as they arrived at the site that it was bad news. Over the years she'd been working as a paramedic, she'd developed a sixth sense about these things.

She was never happy to be proved right — and tonight was no exception.

'Over here,' someone called as she and Glenn got out of the ambulance.

The acrid smell of smoke attacked her senses as soon as she was out of the vehicle. Ignoring it and the blazing warehouse, she rushed towards the figure who was waving to attract their attention.

The casualty was lying on the ground,

not moving. A firefighter in full protective uniform.

'Part of the roof collapsed on him. We had to pull him out in a hurry,' one of his colleagues said. 'I only hope we haven't caused more damage by moving him.'

'You couldn't have left him in there,' Laura said reasonably. Her next words died on her lips when she saw who it was.

It was Angus.

'Keep still.' She placed gentle hands on his shoulders and held him to the ground. 'Don't move until we know the extent of any injuries.'

He was unconscious by the time they got him into the ambulance. A mixed blessing. It was always easier to move a patient in that state — but the major worry was of what damage had been done to bring that condition about.

They wouldn't know for sure until they got him to hospital and the staff there would be able to give him scans and x-rays. They handed him over and Laura was confident he was in good hands. But this was another patient she would have to check up on once her shift was over.

'Do you think we'd better let your sister know?' Glenn asked once they were on their way back to the fire.

'Mmm. That thought had occurred.'

Laura daren't even try to guess how Flora would react to the news that Angus had been hurt.

'It's my fault,' she said almost to herself.

'What's your fault?'

'Flora's going to lose someone else she cares about and it's my fault. I encouraged her to go out with him. I told her to be brave.'

She knew she'd gone too far. She shouldn't be involving Glenn in this. And she knew her fear was irrational.

'We don't have any reason not to hope he'll make a full recovery,' Glenn said quietly. 'We must always think positive. There's every chance he'll be OK.'

'I should have stayed out of it. Her love life is none of my business.'

'You're her sister. You want her to be happy.'

She turned the blue lights on and put her foot down on the accelerator. They needed to get back to the fire quickly — in case there were any other casualties.

'Besides,' he carried on, 'nobody could ever think what's happened tonight is your fault.'

'Maybe not. But even if nobody else blames me, I blame myself that I encouraged Flora to care for a man with a dangerous occupation.'

Laura spent her entire life worrying about Fraser being injured at work. She should have known better.

How was she going to tell Fraser that his best friend had been badly hurt? How was she going to tell her sister that her boyfriend might not recover?

★ ★ ★

When Laura finally returned home, as it turned out, she didn't need to tell Fraser — one of his and Angus's colleagues had already been to the flat to fill him in on the situation.

208

'They think it was a deliberate fire, too,' Fraser said, his face pale.

She sat down next to him on the sofa.

'Has there been any more news?' she asked anxiously.

'He's still hanging in there.'

'That's good.'

Fraser acknowledged that fact with a short nod.

'We need to tell Flora,' he said.

What he really meant was that she needed to tell Flora. She wasn't looking forward to it — but she knew she needed to get over there before the news spread and she heard it from someone else. Someone who might be careless with the facts and worry her more than was even necessary.

'Fraser?'

'What is it?'

'Will you come with me to tell Flora? I wouldn't ask, but I really don't know how she'll take it. We may need someone to distract the girls — make their breakfast, take them out to the garden. . .'

He was on his feet before she'd even

finished speaking.

'Let's go now. It's not fair to keep her hanging on.'

* * *

When Flora saw Laura and Fraser on her doorstep, the blood drained from her face.

'It's Angus, isn't it?' She swayed and held on to the door jamb for support. 'I knew as soon as I heard the local news. They said a firefighter had been injured and I just knew it would be him.'

'Come on, let's get inside.' Laura took Flora's arm and guided her into the kitchen where she made her sit down. There was no sign of Amelia and Jessica. 'Where are the girls?'

'At a sleepover. A girl from their class has a birthday.'

'When will they be back?'

'Not until later this afternoon. Look, tell me, please. I have to know. How bad is it?'

Laura could have sugar-coated it. She

could have taken the easy option and given platitudes and vague answers that would have told Flora nothing. But her sister deserved better than that.

'It's bad.'

'Oh.'

Laura was aware of Fraser putting the kettle on and going about the ordinary business of finding cups and spoons so he could make tea. And she was glad she'd asked him to come.

It might seem odd to rely on an ex-husband to such an extent, especially an ex-husband who would soon no longer be a part of her life, but while he was here, while they were still friends, she needed his strength to help her through this.

She needed his support to help her be strong for her sister. Particularly when she was about to drown in guilt for having been the one to encourage the relationship between Flora and Angus.

'Is he . . .? Will he . . .?' Flora took a deep breath, steeling herself for the unspeakable question. 'Will he live?'

As a professional, Laura never made promises she couldn't keep. She never lied to patients or their families — even if the answers were difficult to hear.

She sat down opposite Flora, took her sister's cold hands in her own, and looked her straight in the eye.

'I don't know,' she said. 'But I promise you he's in good hands. I know these doctors and nurses. They will do everything they can for him.'

Flora nodded.

Fraser brought the tea over. This was turning out to be his speciality — hot, sweet tea in a crisis.

Unfortunately, these occasions where tea was required were turning out to be far too frequent.

'Do you think I could go and see him?'

Laura exchanged a quick glance with Fraser — his nod was almost imperceptible.

'Sure, why not,' she said. 'Though there's no guarantee they'll let us in.'

They drove in silence and, when they reached the hospital, it seemed they would be sent away once they admitted they weren't relatives.

'His family aren't local,' Flora said when they were asked. 'I'm his girlfriend,' she added. 'Does that make a difference?'

It seemed it did.

'OK, wait here,' the nurse instructed. 'We'll let you know if there's any news.'

Laura tried to ignore how weird it felt to hear Flora describing herself in such terms. She hadn't been anyone's girlfriend in years, and she hadn't been going out with Angus that long.

'I feel a fraud,' Flora admitted, seeming to have read Laura's thoughts. 'We've only been going out five minutes. We haven't even had the boyfriend-girlfriend talk yet. As far as I know he might just look on me as his friend. What if he's offended that I've said that?'

That was when Laura knew for sure that despite Laura telling her sister the situation wasn't good, Flora was ignorant of the true nature of Angus's injury. If she fully realised how serious it was, offending him would be the last thing she'd be worried about.

She knew she should put her sister in the picture and she opened her mouth to do so, but Fraser caught her eye and imperceptibly shook his head.

She closed her mouth again, recognising that he was right. She wasn't a doctor. Telling Laura to expect the worst would achieve nothing.

'Nonsense. He won't be offended.' Fraser put an arm around Flora's shoulder and gave her a quick hug.

'What will I do if he doesn't wake up?' she asked then. Laura realised that maybe the extent of Angus's injuries hadn't escaped her after all.

'You mustn't think like that,' Fraser said. 'We can't second guess his condition. The doctors will let you know when they have a better idea of what's going on. There's no point in worrying before we know.'

His tone calmed the situation instantly and Flora nodded.

Laura was so glad that he'd come

along. She was an expert in keeping calm and soothing the worries of relatives, but only when they were someone else's relatives, it seemed. Flora was a bit too close — when her sister was hurting, she was hurting, too. It was impossible to remain detached from that.

'I'll go and fetch us some coffee,' Laura offered, knowing there was no telling how long the wait would be.

'Are you putting me out of a job?' Fraser joked.

Laura tried to smile, but it all fell a bit flat with the mood in the waiting room at the moment.

'Easier for me to carry three plastic cups from the vending machine,' she told him. 'My ankles are both in tip-top condition.'

'OK.' He took a seat near the window. 'No need to brag.'

Flora sat beside him. Their attempts to keep the conversation light for her benefit seemingly lost on her.

'Thanks, Laura.' She turned to stare through the window.

Laura wasn't gone long, but when she returned, Flora was no longer there.

'Where is she?' She handed a plastic cup of nondescript liquid to Fraser and watched him wince as he took a drink.

'Oh, that's vile.'

'Where's Flora?' she asked again.

'They came to get her.'

'What did they say? How's Angus?'

'They didn't say much. He's regained consciousness and was asking for her. Just as well we came.'

Laura nodded, putting Flora's coffee safely on to the windowsill to await her sister's return.

'Well, that's good. It's very positive that he was alert enough to ask for Flora.'

He nodded.

'And how are you doing?' she asked. The fact that Angus was a friend and a colleague of Fraser's hadn't escaped her. In his own way, he was every bit as close to Angus as she was to Flora.

'Bearing up,' he said. His expression contradicted the words.

'Really?'

'It's tough, you know, when it's one of your own. We all feel it when one of the team has been injured — especially when it's as serious as Angus's accident.'

'He's more than a part of the team, though, isn't he? He's your friend.'

Fraser nodded, as though the words were too much for him.

Laura reached out and put her hand on his arm.

'I'm sorry,' she said.

He didn't reply, but he reached up and covered her hand with his own.

They sat there for what seemed like an age, neither wanting to move. Laura was exhausted to the bone — worn out by her shift and the trauma of having to deal with a casualty she knew, someone who meant a lot to members of her family.

It seemed the most natural thing in the world to rest her head on his shoulder.

She wasn't asleep when Flora came back, but her eyes were closed and it was only when Fraser straightened up in his chair she was alerted to the fact that her

217

sister was standing in front of them.

She took in her sister's pale face and red nose and eyes. Flora hardly ever cried. This wasn't good at all.

'What did the doctor say?' she asked as she got to her feet and went to hug Flora.

Flora gave a loud sniff.

'They're still assessing him, but they say he's been very lucky, but oh, Laura — he's very poorly. He could barely talk.'

'The medication will have made him groggy,' Laura said.

Flora nodded, then buried her head in Laura's shoulder before the floodgates opened.

Laura let her cry. Crying was the best therapy in the world but she also knew that Flora's worries wouldn't be over when the tears dried. There was no telling at this stage, until the doctors had made a full assessment exactly what Angus — and Flora — would be facing in the coming weeks and months.

But, as she'd said to Fraser earlier, the fact he had been able to ask for Flora was a good sign. As was the fact they had told Laura that Angus had been lucky.

★ ★ ★

'I can't believe this is happening,' Flora said when they were back in her kitchen a little later.

The doctors had decided they needed to operate — there was internal bleeding that wouldn't wait and, later, bones that would need to be pinned — and there had been no prospect of Flora being allowed in to see him any time soon, so Fraser and Laura had eventually managed to persuade her to come home.

'He'll be OK,' Fraser insisted, refusing to believe anything else.

He wasn't given to fanciful daydreaming, but positive thinking was all he had right now. And Angus deserved that.

The sound of the front door opening had them all looking at each other — bound by a moment of surprise.

'Flora?' It was Nancy's voice.

'Mum — we're in the kitchen,' Laura

called, and a moment later her parents descended on them.

'Oh, my darling.' Nancy hugged her elder daughter tightly. 'We came as soon as we heard. I'm glad you're here,' she reached out and held Laura's hand, 'looking after your sister.'

Drew Robertson, at the best of times a man of few words, engulfed the three women in a giant bear hug.

Fraser sat by awkwardly and watched the scene unfold. He knew Angus hadn't been a part of their lives in any major way for very long, but they were obviously worried about him. And he was glad his friend had that kind of support.

It was pretty obvious they were also worried about Flora.

He wondered what he should do. He was out of his depth. This was definitely not a place for him. This was a close-knit family and, for the time when they'd been married, they had welcomed Fraser into their hearts.

They were still lovely to him — as evidenced by his treatment after he and

220

Grace had gone to stay with Laura — but that part of his life was over now and by staying he was intruding on a private family matter.

Besides, he hadn't really had the opportunity to get his head round what had happened to Angus. Laura had been right — Angus was his friend as well as his workmate and he was struggling with the fact they still didn't know for sure the full extent of his injuries, or how likely he was to make a full recovery.

These things were a real wake-up call. Every call they attended could be their last. They all knew it, though it was something Fraser tried not to dwell on.

In addition to Angus's injury they had to face the fact there might be a criminal running around town, setting fire to buildings.

Knowing it might have been deliberate, made the fire that had caused Angus harm seem so much worse.

He struggled to his feet.

'I'll get out of your way and call myself

a cab,' he said, excusing himself from the group.

There was a chorus of objections, even though he knew they'd all be OK because they had each other.

'I promised I'd go and see how Kim is doing.'

Laura made to get to her feet.

'I'll take you.'

He put a hand on her arm to still the movement.

'I'll be fine.' He smiled into her eyes. 'I'm a big boy and I can take care of myself.'

'But your ankle ...'

'I'm getting better,' he assured her, 'and I'll have the cab drop me off at the door. It won't be under any stress.'

By detaching himself from this strong family unit, he was beginning his retreat from the make-believe world he'd lived in with Laura for the past few weeks.

She hadn't mentioned moving away recently, and she hadn't mentioned the interview she'd been to, but the fact she wanted to move away from Tighnamor was always there at the back of his mind.

He'd sensed her withdrawing from him ever since Grace had gone home. And he was helpless to stop her.

Decisions

Even though she knew she would see him later, Laura was jolted by Fraser's departure. She had grown so accustomed to having him nearby when she wasn't on duty. She'd known all along it wouldn't last for ever, but it was still a shock that he was no longer at her side.

She made all the right comforting noises for Flora — and her heart was breaking for her sister. On the brink of happiness with a new romance, Angus's accident really was the most rotten luck all round.

'I was worried,' Flora said as she sat with Laura and their mother, 'that I was daft to try dating again. That I'd never meet another man I could care about. And as soon as I let my guard down and meet someone nice, this happens.' She sniffed.

Laura went to hug her sister, but their mother beat her to it.

And it suddenly hit her. Flora was

being well supported by their parents. It was Fraser who needed her.

His friend had been injured. At the moment, they didn't know if he would live or die. And if he did, please God, survive, they didn't know how life-changing any injuries might be.

Their parents would stay tonight and take care of the girls and be a shoulder for Flora. But if Laura stayed here, Fraser would be on his own.

The family barely noticed as she said her goodbyes and left.

She drove straight round to Kim's. Fraser would still be there — it wasn't that long since he'd left.

The blinds at Kim's house were wide open. She could see in quite clearly — and what she saw was another family. A supportive family gathered around Fraser, offering advice and comfort and reassurance.

And that was when she realised with a jolt that she wasn't needed around here either. Fraser had his support system just as Flora had hers. In a way Laura had already removed herself from them. She had mentally prepared to move on and now that she had her job offer, the final piece was in place.

With a sigh, she went up the path and rang the doorbell. Now she was here, she might as well see if Fraser wanted a lift back. He might well want to stay here tonight but, if he didn't, she disliked the thought of him struggling back to the flat.

Besides, she was used to being useful, and she wasn't about to stop the habit of a lifetime just because her heart was breaking at the prospect of leaving him for ever.

'Come in,' Kim greeted her with a smile. 'I take it you've come to collect my big brother?' Then she leaned in closer so she could speak a little more quietly. 'I'm really worried about him. I've never seen him so affected by a colleague's accident.'

'Angus is a close friend,' Laura replied. 'The accident is bound to hit the entire crew hard, but especially Fraser.'

He smiled when he saw her, but she noticed the lines of stress around his eyes. At the hospital and at Flora's he'd held his emotions together, but here, with his family, he'd let his true feelings out. That's what you did with family.

The smile he mustered for her, the front he was putting on that he hadn't felt he needed to with Kim and her husband, proved that he no longer considered her close enough to allow his guard down in times of stress.

Which was good because, even if it was for the greater good, how could she have left Tighnamor if Fraser had still thought of her as family?

Now she knew beyond doubt she was doing the right thing, she felt strangely numb.

The sooner she made her new start the better. But she wouldn't tell him tonight. Tonight she would be the friend he needed.

But only for tonight.

As soon as they knew more of how Angus was doing — when hopefully there was positive news — she would tell him about her job offer and confirm her decision to move away.

★ ★ ★

Fraser was touched beyond reason that Laura had come to fetch him from Kim's house.

'I could have phoned for a taxi,' he told her as got into the car. 'You didn't need to bother picking me up.'

He was finding it much easier to get around now — his injuries were healing nicely and without the baby and all her paraphernalia to cart around he wasn't nearly as restricted as he had been.

His pleasure at seeing Laura at Kim's was more to do with spending time with her than it was to do with ease of transportation.

'I know I didn't have to.' She glanced at him from the driver's seat. 'But I wanted to.'

Since Grace had gone, she'd been more distant. He'd been so sure he'd lost her again. But they both missed Grace — it was only natural when the baby had been so much a part of their lives and her departure had been so sudden.

With this one thoughtful gesture, picking him up when she didn't need to, was she maybe also hoping for a reconciliation? He was reminded of the morning she had come by A&E after her shift to give him a lift. He'd been hopeful then, too.

Given she was driving him towards her flat and still hadn't suggested he go back to his house he reasoned he had more than enough cause for optimism.

Maybe, he dared to hope, the time they'd spent together these past few weeks had shown her that they could be happy. That the arguments were in the past and they had both matured. And perhaps the time they had spent with Grace might have shown her how a baby could fit into their busy lives and that they would be good parents.

But now, when they were worried about Angus, when Laura was worried about how her sister was coping, wasn't the time to discuss such things.

It seemed the time was never right.

But there was some news to share with her. As she pulled into her parking space and turned off the engine, he cleared his throat.

'The chief called before you arrived at Kim's. They've made an arrest over the fires on the industrial estate,' he told her, knowing she'd be interested. She'd attended two of those fires herself and would have known how serious the crimes had been.

She sat up in her seat, all eyes.

'Who is it?' She demanded.

'A disgruntled ex-security guard. He was sacked for falsifying his references, and he decided to take revenge.'

'Nobody we know?'

He shook his head.

'Why? Why would anybody do something like that?'

'He has issues. Hopefully now he's been arrested he will be dealt with and get the help he needs.'

'That's all very well, but he could have killed someone.' Her face was pale. 'Angus.'

The same thought had occurred to him, but it didn't do to dwell on what might have happened — which was ironic when that's all he had been doing lately where Laura was concerned.

'Or you.' The whisper reached out to him and she was even paler now as that possibility sunk in. 'He could have killed you.'

'But he didn't. I'm fine. And Angus will be fine. He has to be.'

She nodded.

'It's going to make a big mark on Tighnamor for years to come,' he said seriously. 'There will be a lot of rebuilding required on the industrial estate, for a start.'

She sighed.

'Buildings can be replaced. But three firefighters have been injured.'

'And two of us are fine, and the third one is getting the best possible care.'

Once in her flat, she made tea and

231

they sat together at the kitchen table.

He was glad he was here. He would have hated to sit on his own tonight. That was one of the things he missed most about being married to her — having someone he felt was on his wavelength by his side in times of trouble.

His own accident had taught him how fragile the human body was. Even though it had been minor in the scheme of things, it had made a big impression. He'd always been strong and active — and one daft landing off a ladder had rendered him virtually helpless.

Nobody was invincible. Not even a firefighter at the peak of physical and mental fitness. It was a sobering thought.

She reached out a tentative hand and as her fingers touched his, he offered a hesitant smile. He needed the comfort her touch offered, and she seemed to pick up on that, curling her hand around his.

If things were different, if they weren't so worried about their friend, he could have sat here with her until the end of time.

When Laura's phone rang, they both jumped, startled by the sudden noise that broke the silence.

'It's Flora,' she told him as she accepted the call, then spoke into the handset.

'Is there any news?'

It seemed like a lifetime before she said anything. He could hear Flora's voice but couldn't make out her words.

Eventually Laura smiled.

'That's really good news,' she told her sister.

He let out a breath he hadn't even realised he'd been holding.

She was still smiling as she put the phone down.

'Angus is out of surgery. It went well. They're hopeful he'll make a full recovery.'

'Thank goodness.' It was only then he realised how tense he'd been waiting for news.

She got up and walked around the table and he got to his feet to meet her. She enfolded him in her arms. Gratefully, he clung to her. Hand holding was no longer enough. The events of the past few hours made him crave the human contact a hug afforded.

He lost track of how long they stood like that, neither moving, before she spoke.

'They offered me the job.'

She blurted the words against his neck as she hugged him, and he tightened his arms around her.

He felt rather than heard her sharp intake of breath after she'd told him. He knew that sharing the news must have been difficult for her.

'I'm taking it as a personal insult that you're moving so far away.'

His attempt at humour was to make her feel better and he smiled to soften the words — even though he had never felt less like smiling.

He would finally have to let her go and any hopes of a reconciliation along with her.

'I think we need to talk,' she said.

He couldn't imagine what else there

was left to say and she seemed reluctant to speak — to tell him what she apparently felt she needed to say.

'You want me to let you go.' He said it for her — a blurted out phrase with no forethought and no planning but words that he thought encapsulated everything she couldn't bring herself to say.

'You want to move away with no fuss. You don't think we should see each other again.'

She seemed shocked by the harsh brutality of the words said out loud.

The colour left her face and her pallor made him wonder, for just an instant, if maybe he had misjudged the situation. But that was probably wishful thinking on his part.

He'd tried not to sound bitter. Not to sound as though his heart was breaking in two. They were no longer married and there was no reason for them to ever have any contact again.

'We were only supposed to be apart a short while.' She sounded on the verge of tears and he held her closer.

He remembered the plan well. She was going to help her newly widowed sister who was struggling to hold things together for her twin daughters.

'We'd been arguing.' He frowned. 'Like a lot of newly-weds do.'

'I know. It seemed easier for me to get my own place once Flora was ready for me to leave. I was just so tired.'

He could believe it. Flora had understandably been a mess of raw emotion. They'd all been exhausted.

'I always meant to move back,' she admitted. 'Once that awful time was over, but somehow weeks turned into months, then to years. . .'

'I let you down.' He'd been too immature to know what to do. But he wasn't so young now. 'If you gave me another chance I'd be a better husband.'

She opened her mouth, but didn't speak. Shocked that he'd guessed what she had to say?

She took a deep breath.

'Is that what you want? Another chance?'

'You must know it is.'

She let out a breath that might have been a sigh of relief. Gave a brief nod.

'It's what I want, too.'

Hope, the cursed feeling that always sprang to life around her at the slightest provocation, began to flutter in his heart again.

'What did you say?'

'I don't want to leave you, Fraser. That wasn't why I said we needed to talk.'

Spoken so quietly that he took a moment to gather his wits and take in what she had actually said.

But she had definitely said it. She had said the words he had longed to hear so many times during the past years. He was aware of the upward curve of his lips as pure joy rushed through him.

And she smiled back.

But there was still a hesitation — a reserve that he had no idea how to break down the defences she'd so successfully kept in place over the past few years.

As her smile faded, he could see an

anxious gleam in her eyes.

'What is it, Laura?'

'Have we left it too late? Do you think we might have thrown away our chance to be happy together?'

'Absolutely not,' he told her, adamant that he spoke the truth.

'What about the arguments? What if we find we can't agree on anything again?'

If that was her only worry, he could put it easily to rest.

'This time we'll work things out,' he insisted. 'Parting seemed the easy option last time, but now we know how difficult it really was we will be more careful with our relationship.'

She nodded and he gathered her close.

'I won't be so careless,' he clarified. 'Or thoughtless. And if I do mess things up, I'm going to rely on you to put me right. To tell me what you need from me.'

She was crying now and he gently brushed away her tears with the back of his fingers.

'Happy tears,' she insisted.

And he could understand that because he felt like crying, too.

'Will you marry me?' he asked. 'Again.'

'Yes.' She didn't even hesitate for a heartbeat before she gave her answer. 'Yes, Fraser, I will.'

'So, what are we going to do?' he asked. 'You're going to be living hundreds of miles away. And I live here.'

'I haven't accepted the London job, or given notice here. I'll stay in Tighnamor,' she decided.

That was certainly the option that made the most sense. They both had family and friends here. But she had really wanted this job and he knew her career was important to her.

'Or I could move south with you.'

She sprang back, with a frown on her lovely face. 'You'd do that? Leave Tighnamor? Leave your family? For me?'

'Don't you know by now that I'd do anything for you?' He meant it.

She grinned.

'And I'd do anything for you. I'm going

239

to turn the job down. We both belong in here.'

His arms tightened around her and, as she lifted her face for his kiss, he knew he'd never let her go again.

We do hope that you have enjoyed reading this large print book.

Did you know that all of our titles are available for purchase?

We publish a wide range of high quality large print books including:
Romances, Mysteries, Classics
General Fiction
Non Fiction and Westerns

Special interest titles available in large print are:
The Little Oxford Dictionary
Music Book, Song Book
Hymn Book, Service Book

Also available from us courtesy of Oxford University Press:
Young Readers' Dictionary
(large print edition)
Young Readers' Thesaurus
(large print edition)

For further information or a free brochure, please contact us at:
Ulverscroft Large Print Books Ltd.,
The Green, Bradgate Road, Anstey,
Leicester, LE7 7FU, England.
Tel: (00 44) **0116 236 4325**
Fax: (00 44) **0116 234 0205**

Other titles in the
Linford Romance Library:

THE SUMMERHOUSE GHOST

Camilla Kelly

Lizzie is thrilled when her theatre company gets the chance to put on an open-air production at a Georgian country house. As soon as she sees the property she's enchanted by it – and by two of the residents: Griffin, and his foster son, Oscar. But the house has secrets, and something within it starts to threaten the play, Lizzie's new relationships, and her safety. Something in the house wishes her harm …